Zombies Don't Date

Decomposed by R. W. Zander

SCHOLASTIC INC.

NEW YORK TORONTO LONDON AUCKLAND SYDNEY
MEXICO CITY NEW DELHI HONG KONG BUENOS AIRES

If you purchased this book without a cover, you should be aware that this book is stolen property. It was reported as "unsold and destroyed" to the publisher, and neither the author nor the publisher has received any payment for this "stripped book."

No part of this publication may be reproduced in whole or in part, or stored in a retrieval system, or transmitted in any form or by any means, electronic, mechanical, photocopying, recording, or otherwise, without written permission of the publisher. For information regarding permission, write to Scholastic Inc., Attention: Permissions Department, 557 Broadway, New York, NY 10012.

ISBN 0-439-39869-X

Copyright © 2003 by By George Productions. All rights reserved. Published by Scholastic, Inc. SCHOLASTIC and associated logos are trademarks and/or registered trademarks of Scholastic, Inc.

12 11 10 9 8 7 6 5 4 3 2 1   3 4 5 6 7 8/0

Printed in the U.S.A.   40

First printing, December 2003

CHAPTER ONE

Maybe someday, I won't have a million things going wrong all at once. But today is not that day.

That's the thought that was running through my head as I got dressed that morning. I was already late, and my mom was yelling up the stairs at me: "Amber, we're supposed to be at the mall in ten minutes. Are you almost ready?"

I wanted to make the woman happy. I really did. I did promise to make a trip to the mall just so she wouldn't feel so bad about having a soccer-playing tomboy for a daughter. But when I looked out the window, I saw a zombie chasing my friend Zack Margolis around. And I had to do something to help him.

Yes, you heard me right: a zombie. As in the walking undead. A few weeks ago, Zack took a dare and went to the cemetery in the middle of the night, and four dead bodies crawled out of their graves to follow him home. Now they live in the tunnels under his house. The tunnels were built in the 1800s to hide slaves escaping to the North. But they make great zombie hiding places, too.

Zack is a great guy. He's trying to adjust to living here in Paxituckett, Pennsylvania. He didn't want to move here from Florida. He's really shy, too. The last person you'd figure for a zombie catcher.

But right now, I saw Zack chasing a zombie around his yard. It was Chastity. Her skirts flew as she ran, holding something away from him. Zack's little brother, Tyler, chased her. For him, it was just a crazy game of tag.

"Amber! I need you down here, dressed, RIGHT NOW!" Mom called.

"Chastity, please. That belongs to my sister, and I have to get it back into her room!" Zack's voice floated up from the yard.

My mom was having a fit. But Zack looked totally freaked out. Now I could see what Chastity was holding. A shiny fairy wand that Zack's older sister kept on her bureau. Totally stupid. The kind of thing my mother always gives me.

In fact . . .

I dug through my junk drawer until I found

what I needed: a pink mask covered in sequins. Part of a Halloween costume I was supposed to wear. (I had been planning to be a zombie, but that didn't seem so funny anymore.) Anyway, it was just the thing to distract Chastity.

"Hey! Zack!" I leaned out my window, waving the mask. "Yo! Look up here!"

He couldn't hear me. I had no choice. My mom was yelling, but my friend was in trouble. Help or mall? Well, what would you do?

"I just need five more minutes, Mom! Sorry," I called downstairs. Then I swung myself out of the window and into my tree house. My dad built it before my parents got divorced. It makes the perfect secret entrance and exit to my room. I climbed down the ladder and raced across the backyard, waving the mask like a flag.

"Chastity!" I called. "Check this out! Isn't it cool?"

The zombie girl stopped in her tracks and stared at the mask. The sparkles glinted in the sun. Chastity beamed.

"Give me that," she demanded.

"Nah-ah-ah!" I held it back. "First, you give me that magic wand."

She looked at the wand, then back at the

mask. What a choice: the useless or the totally stupid? This girl was a sucker for frilly junk.

"I want the mask," she decided.

"Come this way, and I'll give it to you." I dangled the mask from the pink ribbons that hung from it. She reached for it. Keeping it just out of her reach, I led her toward the basement door of Zack's house.

I shoved open the cellar door and felt the cool, earthy air of the zombies' favorite place. "Okay, here," I said, grabbing the wand out of Chastity's hand.

She put the mask over her face. "What a lovely mask," she said, smoothing the sequins with her rotting fingers. Her nails were black at the edges and falling off in places. It made me shudder. I'm not scared of the zombies — not the way Zack is. But they aren't exactly cuddly.

I slammed the door on Chastity and turned to Zack, who was just coming up behind me. He was holding his little brother's hand. Tyler grinned. Zack looked a little pale under his freckles.

"Here you go, bud," I told him, handing him the wand. "It's as good as new, except for the stench of death."

Zack didn't smile. He just handed the wand

to Tyler and ran a hand through his brown hair. "I can't take it anymore."

Just then Kyle Jackson came up. He's our third partner in zombie wrangling. Some kids say he's a dead ringer (ha-ha) for Will Smith from *Men in Black II*. Those movies brought together Kyle's love for freaky events and his need to look like the coolest guy in the world. He actually wears a sport coat and tie — and those shades. Girls love him. Teachers stare at him.

Kyle is the perfect guy to have around when rotting corpses are infesting your basement. Before we ever met a single zombie, he had a fat notebook called the Freaky Files. That's where he took notes on every movie, every book, every Web site that mentioned freaky things. Kyle has it all — vampires, space men, werewolves, ghosts, goblins, creepy critters, scary monsters, witches, warlocks, and, of course, zombies.

Those notes have come in mighty handy, let me tell you.

"I've got my video camera," he said. "I want to interview all the zombies to add to my files."

"That's a great idea," I said. "The only trouble is, it looks like we've got two other creeps to get rid of first."

Over Kyle's shoulder, I could see Parker Tolan and Rick Samuels. Ugh. Think of your school's most annoying bullies, then multiply them by ten.

"Hey, Kyle," Parker said, giving the Freaky Files a slap that sent the notebook tumbling to the ground. The video camera lurched dangerously, but Kyle managed to hang on to it.

"Parker, don't you have some old ladies to harass?" I asked, helping Zack pick up the files. "Or, I don't know, weekend detention or something?"

"Nah, not today." Parker sighed, stretching. "We were just enjoying the sights when we spotted El Dorko here with his notebook."

"Yeah, what are you doing, nerd?" Rick piped up. Imagine a weasel without fur, and you've got Rick. "A little extra studying?"

"Ha-ha," Kyle muttered. I knew he was wishing he could neuralize these guys into smoking piles of organic matter.

Zack stood up. "What do you guys want? You're on my property, you know."

"Oooh, look who got all brave since he went to the cemetery," Parker said mockingly. "You won your bet, dorkface. I just want to know when you're going to make me pay up. I'm not

6

about to have you run around school saying I welched on a bet."

"Forget it," Zack said. "You don't owe me anything."

See, these two charmers were the ones who dared Zack to go to the graveyard that night. We never settled exactly what they would have to do if Zack came through. I guess we didn't expect it to happen. Zack surprised us all.

Right now, we had to get Parker and Rick out of Zack's backyard. If the zombies showed up, our secret would be out. And we didn't want anyone to know about our undead friends.

"I just — why don't you leave right now, and we'll call it even," Zack said desperately. We could hear thumping from inside the basement. Someone was bound to come stomping out.

"I should have guessed it — the wimp's way out. He can't even come up with a payoff!" Parker cackled, but he was on his way. "I'm not done with you eggheads," he called over his shoulder.

"AMBER!" I heard my mom's voice float out from my bedroom window. Crikey. She still thought I was in my room!

"Gotta go, guys." I started to swing my way up

the tree outside my house. My dog Farley was growling like a tiger. That was weird, but I was in too much of a hurry to worry about it. Farley's usually a mellow dog.

Then I saw why he was barking. Remember, I told you there were three zombies left? One was Chastity Wells, the teenager with a taste for ribbons and bows. One was Penelope, an old lady who started fires. And the other one was Lassiter.

Man, was he a jerk. He used to be some kind of lumberjack. I'm not saying he was unpopular when he was alive, but right now, he's got a big ax hanging out of his back. You do the math.

He hadn't been staying at Zack's house that much. You'd think that would be a relief, but it just made us nervous. He had already hurt a construction worker at the graveyard, and who knew what trouble he was stirring up in town. I did not like this guy at all.

And right now, he was in *my* tree house, staring in *my* bedroom window, glaring at *my* dog. And I know this sounds crazy, but the guy looked downright hungry!

CHAPTER TWO

HEY!" I yelled.

Lassiter jumped, startled. The ax in his back wiggled as he turned to face me. His breath almost knocked me backward, but I stood my ground.

"Were you going to eat my dog?" I accused him, sticking my finger in his ugly, half-rotten face.

"What? Eat your — HA!" His bearded mouth twisted into a sneer. "You stupid girl. If I wanted to eat your dog, I would have done it already." Then he leaned in close, giving me a personal view of his rotting face. Leathery skin covered his missing eye. The other eye gleamed, a network of red veins. "There'd be nothing left of him but a tail and a collar."

To tell you the truth, I was quivering inside. This guy wasn't right in the head. But there was no way I was going to let him know how scared I was.

"Then why are you staring into my window? You're obviously spying on me. Why don't you just talk to me instead of sneaking around like a coward?"

Lassiter didn't like that. I guess even a *stupid girl* can wound a guy's pride.

He waggled a finger in my face. "Where is Jeremiah?" he asked. "That boy guarded the graveyard like the Civil War was still going on. And now . . . there's no sign of him. What did you do with him? Toss him off a roof so his limbs turned to dust?"

"Only you would think of doing something so mean," I said, though I wondered if that would really work. "We just helped him go to the next world."

"The what?"

I shrugged. "You know. Eternal rest. Beyond. Out there somewhere. We got him out of his body so he could stop roaming the earth."

It was true. Jeremiah was a nice guy, for a zombie, but he wasn't happy in his undead state. We helped him solve his most nagging problem, and — whammo! — he had gone off in a poof. Vanished! Would it work for the rest of the zombies? Kyle thought so, and he was the expert. We figured we could fix each zombie problem and send them off to never-never land. Right?

Easier said than done. The trouble was, it took a lot of time. Plus, Jeremiah had worked with us, and this guy Lassiter was definitely not a team player.

"You destroyed him!" Lassiter growled. "What power do you have? How did you do it?"

I wasn't about to tell him. Suddenly, it was clear that I had something he wanted — information. Maybe he would do what I wanted while I had the upper hand.

"That's for me to know and you to find out — maybe," I said. "I'm not telling you a thing."

Lassiter reared back and roared.

My stomach turned inside out with fear. Inside my room Farley was barking like crazy. *Hold on, Farley*! I thought. This jerk will be gone soon.

"Well, don't try your hocus-pocus on me!" Lassiter shouted. "I like this world. I'm glad your pipsqueak friend woke me. There's so much to do here with your new machinery. A backhoe, for instance. I amused myself last night by learning how it worked."

"What, you've been riding around on construction rigs?" I asked.

"Riding around? I destroyed a small building," Lassiter bragged. "It seems I have a talent for using these destructive machines. And if you get in my way, I will use them to run over your precious dog — or you!"

I *knew* this guy was going to be trouble. I wasn't sure if he'd really smush me with a backhoe, but I didn't want to find out. For now, though, I couldn't show him any fear.

I took a deep breath. "Try it, and you'll regret it. Now, you get your big, rotten self down into those tunnels, or I'll whisk you into the Great Beyond so fast it'll make your head spin!"

"I don't think you will," Lassiter shot back. He looked at me as if he was trying to figure out if I could really do anything to him.

The fact was, I couldn't. I was totally bluffing. The only reason we got Jeremiah to move on with his life — I mean, his death — was because he had wanted to go. He was totally willing. Unlike Lassiter.

But I kept up my bluff. I crossed my arms and glared at him the same way I glare at opposing players on the soccer field. You don't want to mess with my game face.

Lassiter couldn't make me crack, and that

made him mad. He roared and bashed his fists against the tree limbs around him, shaking the branches like crazy. I'm telling you, if I pulled a fit like this dude, I'd be grounded for a week.

Forget the game face. It was time to get out of there.

I backed out of the tree house and slipped a leg over a big branch. My plan was to swing down before he could toss me over the edge.

But just as I started to move, something weird happened.

Lassiter grabbed the shoulder of my jersey with one big, bony hand, and stretched the other one in front of my face. He let out an explosive breath of air.

And the next thing I knew, I was ... *paralyzed*.

It was the most horrible thing. I was totally frozen ... trapped in my body!

Lassiter let go of me, and I slumped across the branch. My legs were still wrapped around it, but my head dangled at an awkward angle. I couldn't move my arms to grab a branch or even steady myself.

My body was asleep.

Lassiter chuckled and climbed out of the

tree. He was in no hurry. He just ambled down like he had all the time in the world.

I tried to shout, but I couldn't say a word. I tried to turn my head, except my head wouldn't listen. All around the edges of my vision, I saw wavery spiderwebs. There was a rushing in my ears like a waterfall. Everything seemed slowed down and dreamlike.

But this was real. I could feel my legs beginning to slip. The autumn breeze was getting colder. I could feel myself shiver inside. But my body didn't move. It couldn't. If I didn't tighten my grip on the big branch soon, I was going to fall. Already my legs were slipping . . . shifting . . . ugh! I was going to break my neck!

Through the whooshing sound, I heard a door slam open.

"Get away from me!" I heard Chastity shout. "It's mine. I found it, and it's mine!"

"It is not yours, it's my sister's," Zack told her. "And I don't think it's a good idea for you to use a hair dryer."

"I must," she insisted. "Leave me to my grooming, you vile boys!"

"Chastity, you hardly have any hair anyway,"

Kyle said. "If you put hot air on it, you're bound to go up in flames."

HEEEELP! I shouted. Except I only shouted in my mind. Nothing squeaked past my frozen lips. *Guys, please find me. Please, find me now,* I wished with all my heart.

"How dare you!" Chastity yelped. "Hardly any hair, indeed. I'll have you know I was voted the prettiest girl in my class, even before I — what on earth! What are you doing up there?" she demanded.

Finally! They'd noticed me.

"Reclining in a tree?" Chastity went on. "Is this another one of these modern habits of yours, like wearing boys' trousers or cutting off your hair? When will you be a lady?"

"Amber?"

I heard Kyle and Zack calling my name. I tried to answer, but nothing came out.

Get up here and help me! I wanted to scream.

"Something must be wrong," Kyle said. "It's not like Amber to shut up about anything."

Zack was already climbing the tree. Kyle swung onto a low branch under him.

Chastity was still fiddling with the dryer.

"Did you not promise me small compensation in exchange for sharing my life story?" she asked. "I demand to know how this air mover fluffs the hair!"

"Would you just shut up?" Kyle snapped at her. She fumed.

Zack reached me first. "Amber? You okay?" I still couldn't answer. "You look like you're going to fall."

I begged him with my eyes. *Please, get me off this branch!*

I don't know if the message was clear, but he seemed to get it. Kyle's face popped up behind him. "I think something's really wrong," Zack said. "She's not moving. Like she turned to stone."

Kyle touched my hand, which slipped an inch or so. "Yeah, she's stuck . . . but . . ."

"Whoa!" Zack shrieked as I started to slip toward the lawn. "Come on!"

The guys tugged me toward the platform. I couldn't help them, but I was so relieved. I was safely off the branch and lying on the wooden-planked floor of my tree house. Zack slapped my cheeks lightly.

"I think she was drooling," Kyle said.

I realized he was right. Gross! This had to be one of the worst days of my life, let me tell you.

"I've flipped the switch," Chastity complained from below. "Yet no air is coming out. Make it work. Zack, please."

Zack totally ignored her. "Amber, wake up," he said. "Hey. What's going on? Kyle, has she ever done this before?"

"No way," Kyle said. "Hang on, let me try something." He yanked open my window, and Farley came charging out.

His muscular body shot toward me like a fur-covered missile. Farley licked my face like it was a giant slab of bacon. I sputtered in response. My arms jerked at my sides, and suddenly I could sit up. My vision cleared, the rushing vanished from my ears, and . . .

"Lassiter!" I said.

"You're back!" Zack responded. "Amber, are you okay?"

"I'm fine, but Lassiter put some kind of whammy on me," I told him. "He pointed at me, and I just froze. I thought I'd never get out of it. And if you guys didn't come along, I would've slipped down to the lawn and cracked in two."

For the first time, Chastity showed interest in

someone other than herself. She pulled herself up into the tree house next to us. "He did?" she asked. "He cast a spell and then didn't undo it? That's odd. It's not supposed to be used that way, but he does write his own rules, that one."

"What do you know about this?" Kyle asked her. "Did he hypnotize Amber? Can you guys do that?"

"Well, it's not considered polite, but yes," she said. "If she's able to move now, that means he's far away — or involved in some other activity that takes his strength away from it."

"That's right," Zack said. "Remember when Jeremiah was rescuing my little brother? He put a whammy on him."

Did I mention that Jeremiah was a good zombie? Yes, he had saved Zack's brother, Tyler, when a tunnel collapsed. But we'd quickly figured out that zombies are as different as . . . well, as people.

"It's still not moving the air!" Chastity said, peering into the vent of the hair dryer.

"Would you give it a rest?" I said. "Sheesh, I just got hypnotized."

"Just what I was saying," Zack went on. "Lassiter put the whammy on you."

"But why was he back here at all?" Kyle asked.

"He was spying," I answered him. "He wanted to find out what power we had. He was scared that we'd figured out how to send Jeremiah away. When I told him it was a secret, he put the whammy on me to make me scared of him."

"I wish we really could just zap them all back," Zack mumbled. "I hate having zombies in my house."

"Yeah, well, in the meantime, we'd better find him before he causes any more trouble," Kyle said.

"You're right," Zack agreed.

"I can't right now. I promised my mom we'd go to the mall." I stuck out my tongue to let the guys know how happy I was about that.

"Dratted machine, why won't you work?" Chastity complained, whacking at the hair dryer with a stick.

"Give me that!" Zack yanked it away from her. "My sister's going to freak if you break it." He turned to me. "Amber, can Chastity stay with you for a while? Last night, she got into Trina's lip glosses, and I got blamed for it. As if I'd ever go near that goop. And I've got my hands full with Penelope. She's probably wrecking the kitchen now."

"She's just trying to bake," Kyle pointed out.

"I know, but she's a total fire hazard," Zack said.

"I'd help you out, but we've got house guests," Kyle said. "Friends of my parents. They've got a little kid who'll be able to see her. I really don't think we want anyone else to meet the walking dead."

That was one of the other zombie traits we'd figured out. For some reason, only kids could see them. As if people lost part of their eyesight when they got older. My mom always says we're on different wavelengths. That was way true.

"Please, Amber?" Zack said. "If Kyle and I go scouting for Lassiter, you're the only one who can take her."

Oh, man. He was right. There was nowhere else to park Chastity for the time being. I was stuck.

"All right, I'll take her," I grumbled. "But you guys had better find Lassiter quickly. We need to get him out of town, or at least out of trouble."

"Thanks, Amber. You're a pal. And hey . . ."

Zack gave me an evil grin. "It's about time you started playing with girls your own age."

"My own age!" I glared at Chastity, who was starting to realize we were talking about her. "She's got a hundred years on me, easy."

"Oh, give her a chance," Kyle said, lowering himself out of the tree. "Maybe she can give you some beauty tips to score points with your mom."

"Ha-ha," I said. I watched them cross the lawn. I turned back to Chastity, who wasn't happy to be stuck with me, either.

The fact was, Kyle had hit a sore point. Chastity was the ultimate girly-girl. She cared about her hair, her clothes, her looks — everything my mom cared about. She was the daughter my mom really wanted.

So that was the beginning of my horrible day. Dodging Mom. Zombie chasing. Getting whammied in my own tree house. Sending my two best friends off to hunt down the baddest zombie ever to hit Paxituckett, Pennsylvania.

And where was I?

Baby-sitting a hundred-year-old spoiled brat!

CHAPTER THREE

What is this odd place?" Chastity asked as she peered into my room from the tree house. "Some sporting club? With all those rackets and balls and what-have-you?"

I thumped open the window and climbed in, annoyed already. Did she have to turn her nose up at everything of mine?

She followed me, the wispy edges of her yellowed dress dragging over the windowsill.

"This is my room," I told her. "And I use those rackets and balls. For soccer and lacrosse and tennis and stuff."

"Certainly you jest!" she told me. "A lady would never do such things, beyond croquet, but only in season."

"Well, *I* do," I said. "Is that so hard to believe? That there might be something more important in life than putting ribbons in your hair and playing dress-up?"

Chastity looked at me like I was the biggest

idiot on earth. Then, before I could stop her, she had yanked open the door to my room and flounced out into the hallway.

I followed her. "Hey, stop! Where are you going?"

"I will not remain in such a dreadful room," she said. "This one is much more to my liking." To my horror, she went right into my mom's room.

As I said, my parents split up about a year ago, and the house is now really feminine. That's Mom's taste. My mom was a beauty queen when she was younger. She even worked as a model for a while, until she met my dad. He's a real-estate developer, like a small-town Donald Trump. They were the golden couple, real head-turners. Except for the fact that they couldn't stand each other.

To tell you the truth, it was a relief when my dad moved out. Mom and Dad spent a lot of time negotiating the divorce, but at least I didn't have to be there for that. And I had soccer season to keep me busy.

Now, my mom's room is like a shrine to all things girly. There is nothing in there that isn't covered with flowers, lace, or pastel colors. I don't know how Mom relaxes in there. All those flowers and frills make my skin itch.

But Chastity felt right at home. She saw the light-blue chenille bedspread, embroidered with a soft yellow sun and white stars, and gasped with joy.

"Oh, rapture!" she squealed, throwing herself on the bed. "Such lovely colors. Oh, it's a canopy bed!"

I knew my mom couldn't see Chastity, but it made me sick to think of her skin flaking off on Mom's prized pillow shams.

"Please get out of here," I begged her.

"Why? It's lovely, like lying on a cloud." Chastity sighed. "When I was alive, I had a feather bed, but it was somewhat lumpy. This bed bounces!" She sat up and sproinged up and down a few times.

"Amber, are you jumping on my bed?" my mom shouted from downstairs. "I told you to be ready to go to the mall. I'm getting into the car and I suggest you join me there, pronto!"

"All right, come here," I said, grabbing Chastity by the arm.

"Ouch! Be careful, or that will come off!" she scolded me. I held on firmly but didn't squeeze.

I'd seen Jeremiah's arm pop off, and it was not pretty. I led her back to my room.

"Look, I have to go with my mom to the mall," I told her. "And I can't deal with you *and* her telling me how bad my clothes are, so you're going to stay here."

Chastity rolled her eyes and sniffed. "You are a rude young lady!"

"Look. Here." I reached under my bed and pulled out an oversized box. I yanked off the top, and Chastity gasped.

"Oh, my!" She dug into the mound of shiny bottles, barrettes, and lacy socks.

It was my junk box, filled with everything girly I had ever received. Tiny perfume samples, bead kits, nail polish, eye shadow, jars of sparkly stuff to decorate T-shirts with. The box held everything a girl could want, if she didn't have a brain.

"All the stuff in this box is yours," I told the zombie. "Go ahead and play with it. I'll be back in a couple of hours, okay?"

"What lovely things!" The mold on her teeth gleamed as she grinned. "Thank you!"

"You're welcome," I said. "At least someone should enjoy it."

"How could you not want such delicate treasures?" She picked up a long strand of seed pearls — a birthday gift from my aunt Lena.

"I asked for soccer cleats," I said.

"My father promised me a trunk full of fine jewelry for my coming-out," Chastity went on. "But I never did reach my eighteenth birthday. Alas, I received naught but the golden locket passed down from my grandmother." She put her long white fingers to her throat as if she could still feel it there. "Oh, how I wish they had buried me in it!"

"Well, now you've got all this junk — er, jewelry," I told her. "So we're all square? You'll be all right?"

She nodded as she traced her finger through the contents of the box. It was like she'd been whomped with her own whammy. She was that hypnotized by the gleaming, glittery girliness in front of her.

I tried to pull a brush through my curly red hair, but it was pointless. I knew my mom would throw a fit if she saw me like that, so I yanked a baseball cap onto my head and bounded down the stairs.

My mom was already waiting in the car. Before I even hit the seat, she was ragging on me.

"My goodness, Amber, you've got tree bark in your hair. Were you rolling around in the dirt?" She pulled the hat off my head, and my frizzy mess tumbled out. "Oh, Amber!" She swatted at my head as if my red hair were a cloud of mosquitoes. "Honestly, would it kill you to take care of your appearance? These are nice shops we're going to."

"Ouch! I don't want to go to any shops," I grumbled.

She gave a sigh and looked out the windshield, as if the answers to her problems would appear like a stop sign. Instead, there was only a yellow sign that said SLOW CHILDREN. Which is what I'm sure she thought she had one of sitting next to her.

We got to the mall and, let me tell you, it was awful. I mean, I'm sure I could have been nicer, but my mom is the grown-up, so she shouldn't have been so mean. First of all, I asked her what this big-deal party was, and she said it was the autumn ball at the country club. And when was it?

Oh, just the same day as my soccer match against the Hurricanes. They're the team we have to beat if we're going to get to the state championships this year.

I know for a fact my coach spoke to Mom about my soccer schedule. She knows this game is important. I dropped the girl gear she had put in my hands and said, "WHAT?"

The saleslady glared at me, and my mom picked up the dresses. "Behave yourself, Amber. You are in public."

"Mom! The date of the party. Don't you remember? It's the day of my huge soccer game."

"You can miss one game," she said.

"It's not one game! It's the biggest, most important one. How can you even ask me to miss it?"

"I'm not asking, I'm telling," my mom insisted. "It's important to keep up appearances."

"Why?" I asked, following her to the next rack. "Why is it so important? Because of Mrs. Ashworth and her snobby friends?"

"I want you to stop discussing this now," she said. "This is no way to behave in public. People know me here!"

"Oh, yeah? Well, people know me, too," I said.

"I'm the starting center on my soccer team and, if I let them down, we can kiss the championship good-bye. That's more important than Mrs. Ashworth!"

"Amber!" Mom glared at me, her eyes blazing with anger. Her voice was quiet, but it was that scary quiet. The "you're in big trouble" voice. "You are going to *take* these three outfits into the dressing room and you are going to Try Them On."

I took the dresses, but I wasn't done. "Why can't I wear pants?"

"You are not wearing pants," she answered. "You wouldn't feel comfortable in casual wear when everyone else is dressed up."

"I'm not going to feel comfortable anyway," I pointed out.

"Young lady, this conversation is over," she stated. "And so is this shopping trip."

Uh-oh. She called me young lady. That meant she was over the edge. The boiling point when you know your mom (who looks calm on the outside) is dangerously close to blowing up. *Ka-blam!*

Sure enough, she took the dresses out of my hand and hung them on the nearest rack. I followed her out of the store, desperately wishing that I had just tried them on. I didn't mean for her to get *this* mad. It just happened.

It all seemed so unfair. I wouldn't — couldn't! — let myself cry. But I couldn't ignore the huge knot forming in my throat. How come my mom got to tell *me* what was important? Why wouldn't she see that I had important things, too? As much as she wants to look good for her friends, I want to win the soccer championship.

We drove home in silence. I crossed my arms and scowled out the window, squishing myself against the door. Meanwhile, my perfect, tall, blonde mother sat there, her knuckles white on the steering wheel. Her mouth was a thin pink line as straight as her spine.

At home, I ran inside and up the stairs, slamming the door to my room behind me. It took me a second to realize what was wrong. In all the arguing with my mom, I had forgotten about Chastity. She was supposed to be in here, but the big box sat abandoned.

Poor Farley looked up at me pitifully. He was wearing most of my jewelry and a bonnet, and even a little makeup on his jowls. There is nothing sadder than a mutt dressed in cheap jewelry.

I knew who was behind the doggie masquerade. But Chastity was nowhere to be found.

Oh, man, what did she do? I wondered. *Where is she? Somewhere in the house?* Before I could figure out what to do next, I heard my mother go past my room and into her own. She slammed the door with as much anger as I felt. There was a moment of silence. And then I heard the words I feared most.

"Amber . . . Amber! WHAT IS GOING ON IN HERE?"

CHAPTER FOUR

Oh. My. Goodness. Chastity must have done something to my mom's room. I tried to imagine the mess: Did she rip Mom's favorite dress so that it would look like her own wispy rags? Did she track dirt on the pink, rose-dotted rug?

Whatever she did, Farley was going to get blamed. And that would be the end of me and my dog. Or maybe Mom would think I somehow ruined her clothes before we left for the mall. And that would be the end of me!

With a thudding heart, I walked down the hall to my mom's room. I saw her standing with her back to me and steeled myself for her angry face. But when she turned to face me, all I saw was a puzzled expression.

"Have you been trying on my clothes?" she asked me. "And my jewelry, too?"

Her words whirled around in my head. I found it hard to answer, because behind her, I saw Chastity. She sashayed out of Mom's walk-in closet and over to the three-way mirror. She was wearing a wild combination: a poofy gold skirt, a ruffled lavender blouse, and a dark green shawl. I guess the zombie girl loved twenty-first century fashion. But even I could tell that she needed help putting it all together.

I wasn't sure what my mom would see if she turned around. Chastity was invisible to adults, like all zombies. But what about the clothes? The sight of waltzing evening wear could really send my mother over the edge. I had to keep her from turning around at all costs!

Luckily, Mom was completely focused on me. I didn't have to do anything. Tears sparkled in her eyes as she came toward me.

"Honey, is that why you didn't want to buy clothes at the mall today? Because you really wanted to wear something of mine? Oh!" She blinked and sucked in her breath. I recognized her I'm-not-going-to-cry mode. "That . . . is so sweet."

She stepped toward me and put her arms around me. Instead of getting yelled at, I was surrounded by a warm embrace and a cloud of her perfume. It was kind of nice.

"I didn't think you liked my things at all," Mom said. "I mean, you never showed any interest before. But if you were trying them on, we can find something for you! It won't fit quite right, but I can have something altered to fit you if you like."

"Or we can check out my stuff," I sputtered, grabbing her hand and yanking her out of her room, away from Chastity. She was so dazed, she didn't even notice. "I . . . I know there's stuff that I've never even worn," I said. "Will you take a look at it, and see if any of it will work for the party?"

"Look at your closet?" She floated down the hall, as happy as if she'd just been crowned Miss America. "Of course!" she said, disappearing into my room.

"Thanks, I'm right behind you." I turned and raced back into her bedroom.

"Chastity? Chastity!" I hissed. The undead diva had wandered back into the closet. Now she was draped in black taffeta. It looked like a funky funeral in there. Around her neck, Chastity had placed a clunky gold necklace with a lion's head medallion. It hung on her skeletal shoulders, looking as if it would crush her fragile frame. I snatched it off her and yanked the black dress away.

"That's it," I spat. Maybe my mom wasn't mad, but I was. "Chastity, you're wrecking everything. This stuff isn't yours!"

She pouted at me with what was left of her bottom lip. "I was just playing," she said. "These things are so pretty. Do you know how dreary and dark everything is underground?"

"Well, it's not a fashion show down there!" I said. "And right now, you have to scram. I have my hands full. You've had your fun, can't you help me out a little?"

From the stubborn look on her face, I had to figure the answer was no.

"All right, look. You love fashion, right?" I asked. Chastity's eyes lit up. "Well, if you head down to the basement right now, you'll find a whole stack of magazines — *fashion books* — in the recycle bin. It's the big blue plastic tub right by the stairs. Can you go down there and read for a while? Please?"

"Very well. But I don't like basements," she reminded me as she creaked down the stairway. "So dreary."

"Well, I don't like you," I muttered, and went back into my room.

Things there had gone from bad to worse. A green plastic bag in the back of my closet held my most hated frou-frou outfits. I thought I had dropped it in the box for the most recent Goodwill drive, but apparently I forgot. Note to self: *Don't ever forget that again*. Because my mom had honed in on that bag like a center heading toward an open goal.

"Look what I found!" she said, rooting through the multicolored contents. "I don't know why you thought there was nothing in here. We must have packed this stuff away for the summer — it's perfect!"

In her hands was the worst thing ever to come out of the missy department at Niederman's Department Store. I think it was someone's idea of a girl's fantasy dress. It was a washed-out pink. The shiny skirt was covered with a bristly netting that made a floofy poof of my lower body. Up top, it had a collar and sleeves of itchy lace, making it the most uncomfortable item of clothing in the history of the world. It was nerdrific in the extreme. If I could have chosen the one thing to burn before she'd find it, that would have been it.

And now Mom was holding it up, delighted.

"Oh," I said. "Wow."

"I know!" my mom said. "It looks just like something I would wear. We'll be a real mother-and-daughter team!"

I swallowed. Oh, this was bad. A mother-and-daughter team? I could just see us in our matching outfits, floating along like two strawberry cupcakes full of helium. But I had to keep her happy.

"All right," I forced myself to say. "I can wear that if you think it would look nice."

"Oh!" Mom was holding the sleeves of the dress, so when she clapped her hands, it looked like the dress was clapping, too. I figured now was the time to make my move.

"So what time does the party start?" I asked.

"Six P.M.," she said.

"Well, Mom, my game is at three. There's time for me to play in my soccer game, come back, change, and get to the party, if I can be a tiny bit late."

Pop! The bubble of happiness disappeared.

My mom looked at me, disappointed. "But, sweetheart, I thought you were excited about the party."

"I am!" I lied. "I'm excited about it. But I still want to play in my soccer game."

"Amber, there's no way we could get ready in time. You'll need to have your hair blown out by Ralph. And I can't get ready myself if I'm driving you all over town."

"Oh, Mom . . ." I felt my control slipping. "That's not true! There'll be time if we do my hair here. I don't have to go to Ralph. I hate that poofy hair, anyway!"

Her whole body stiffened.

I'd stepped over the line.

When my mom spoke again, her voice was quiet. "Sweetie, this is an important party for me. And we are going to do this right, even if it means missing a game. Someday, you'll understand. In the meantime, you're going to this party and you're wearing this dress." She kissed me on the forehead and left my room.

Ugh. UGH!! I wanted to rip the dress to shreds. Instead, I kicked the wall and stubbed my toe. Ow! I flopped to the floor next to Farley, who was jiggling, trying to shake off his jewelry.

I helped him slip out of the bonnet and neck-
laces, then buried my face in his bristly brown
fur.

"I will NEVER understand, no matter how old
I get," I told him. I tried not to cry.

His brown eyes blinked slowly, as if he un-
derstood perfectly. I wished he did understand.
Better yet, I wished I knew how to do the zombie
whammy. That way, I could zap Mom and leave
for the soccer match before she could do anything about it.

Ha! That'd be good!

The thought of whammying my mom almost
made me smile. I calmed down as I rested my
head on Farley's side. I stared at the ceiling, trying to find a way out of this stupid mess. But all I
saw was my ceiling, with its old familiar crack
down the middle and a big blue face.

Big blue face?

Agh! I sat up to get a good look at Chastity.
"What did you do now?" I demanded. Her face
was plastered with a blue goo that I immediately
recognized. It was my mother's facial masque. I
think it costs more per ounce than solid gold.
My mom only uses it for special occasions, and
Chastity was practically swimming in the stuff.

"That stuff is expensive!" I shrieked.

Chastity rolled her eyes. "Well, it's hardly worth it," she declared. "It's certainly not helping to preserve me. I need a real mud bath."

The girl was right. Even behind the masque, I could see her starting to fade. That's another thing about zombies. The mud helps to preserve them. Without it, they dry out superfast. I had to find her some mud, pronto.

"All right, come on," I said, leading her out back, where Mom keeps her gardening supplies. She has big plastic tubs that she uses for planters. Well, I was about to plant my own zombie in one of them: It was the perfect size for Chastity.

"Come on, give me a hand," I said, shoveling dirt into it as quickly as I could. Chastity picked up armloads of dirt and helped me. I guess she was feeling the need for a nice nap, so the dirt didn't bother her.

"I want to get this into the basement," I said. But when I tugged on the handle, I realized it was too heavy to budge. Chastity pushed me aside and grasped it firmly. I forgot: Zombies — even frail, little-girl zombies — have superhuman strength. In the blink of an eye, she toted the tub o' dirt through the double cellar doors. She settled it on the concrete floor of my basement.

"I'll get the hose," I said, but Chastity didn't answer. I looked closely at her. She was really in dire need of her mud bath. Like a starving person, all she could do was stare hungrily at the dirt, anticipating her dive into it and the deep sleep that would restore her. She wasn't really Chastity right now. She was just a zombie, one that needed to regenerate or turn to dust.

I ran up the stairs and got the hose. I felt like a real jerk. While I was arguing with my mom and complaining to Farley about this bratty zombie, I forgot that my job was to take care of her. I double-timed it back down and started splooshing water into the tub.

Chastity shuddered in anticipation.

"Amber!" My mother's voice called down the stairs. "Time to hit the shower and get ready for dinner."

"I'm coming," I squeaked. I stirred the mud a little. This was heavy work, and messy enough that even *I* thought it was gross.

"What are you doing down there?" Mom asked.

"NOTHING!" I yelled. I knew I sounded suspicious. "I mean, I'll be right up," I said.

I heard her pause at the top of the stairs. Then there was a squeak as she started to turn away. The mud was looking great. I was about to tell Chastity to go ahead and sink into it when she gave a hungry roar and leaped in. Mud splattered everywhere as the zombie sank down.

"What was that?" My mom's voice rose about ten notches. Her feet pounded down the stairs.

Here's what she saw: Me, my hair a frizzy mess, covered in mud, holding a running hose in a giant tub of muck.

She gave a shriek that could wake the dead.

CHAPTER FIVE

What do you think you are DOING?" my mother asked, looking like she was about to tear her perfect blonde hair right out of her head. Her face was beet-red, and her blue eyes were as wide as I've ever seen them.

"Mom, keep your shirt on," I said quickly. I reached outside the cellar door and turned off the hose. "I'm just doing a . . . a science project."

Oh, yeah! A science project! I have no idea where that came from, but it just appeared in my brain and popped out of my mouth.

"A science project?" she repeated. "What kind of science project?"

"We have a science fair coming up. I guess I forgot to tell you?" The words tumbled out of my mouth. "So, like, I wanted to show that earthworms can make bad soil into healthy soil. So I took some leftover dirt from the garden and . . . and now I'm making it muddy? And then I'll put the earthworms in? And then they'll make the dirt into healthy potting soil and then after I'm done, you can use it for the window boxes!"

Yikes. I sounded like I was giving a speech at the idiot's convention. No way would she buy it.

"Oh. Worms?" She took a step backward up the stairs. "All right. Well, make sure when you're done, this all gets cleaned up. And take off your clothes before you come up these stairs. I don't want you tracking dirt into the house. I'll leave your bathrobe for you."

With each word, Mom stepped away from the mess, so that by the time she was finished, she was already out of sight. Mud does not go with Gucci loafers.

Of course, this meant I had volunteered myself for the science fair. It's supposed to be only for the geeks who can't get enough of test tubes and litmus paper. I'm horrible at science, and my mom knows it. Now, on top of taking care of zombies, playing soccer, and attending stupid parties, I have to do a science project.

Could my life be a bigger mess?

Oh, well. At least this girly ghoul would be spending the night in the basement and not in my closet.

* * *

The next morning, I met up with Zack and Kyle so we could all walk to school together. I tried to keep my jacket closed, but they were too sharp-eyed for me.

"Look at you!" Kyle said, pulling down his shades so he could look me over.

I was wearing my good old jeans, but on top — Mom's choice. It was a matching sweater-set, embroidered with flowers in a shade that my mother described as "Tiffany's blue." In other words, I looked like a total dorkasaurus.

"Hey, look who's dressing up!" Zack teased. "What happened? Did Chastity pick out your clothes for you?"

"Do not even mention that frosted flake to me," I demanded. "She's a complete and total pain in the neck. And yes, it is her fault I have to wear this stupid thing today. And now that you know about it, let me put my sweatshirt on over it." I stopped and tugged my preferred school-wear over my head.

"Let me tell you about this girl," I said as we strolled to school. "She raided my mom's closet, she dressed up my dog, and her mud bath turned my basement into Disgustoworld."

The guys laughed, which just made me angrier. "I don't know how someone could be a clothes freak and a gross slob at the same time, but she is," I said. "And she's driving me completely crazy. Would you quit laughing?"

"I can't help it," Zack said. "I wish I could've seen Farley all dressed up."

"Well, I wish you had," I answered. "I hated being stuck in the house with a zombie while you guys ran around town having fun."

They exchanged serious looks. "It wasn't all fun and games for us, either," Kyle said.

"So tell me," I said, poking him in the arm.

"We were walking around town and we heard sirens," Kyle explained. "They were heading for the hardware store, so we checked it out."

"Lassiter was there?" I asked.

"No." Zack picked up the story. "But it looked like we just missed him. The owner of the store was totally out of it. He stood behind the counter, frozen. The paramedics were trying to get him to walk it off. We figured Lassiter whammied him."

I shivered, remembering how awful it was to lie there, unable to move or defend myself. The poor guy!

"That's not all," Kyle added. "The store looked like a hurricane had hit it. I'll bet Lassiter tried every power tool in sight. The walls and shelves were wrecked. He made a big L on the wall with the nail gun. And he tried to figure out how to use a leaf blower but ended up throwing it through the window of the store."

"The owner came to as we were standing there," Zack cut in. "The ambulance guys didn't know what to think when he started babbling about the flying power tools."

"Holy-moly," I said. "Lassiter just gets crazier and crazier. We've got to get rid of him — and Chastity and Penelope, too!"

"You said it, sister," Kyle said.

"Well, I'm glad the two of you are starting to see reason!" Zack blurted out. "I knew these cruddy creeps were trouble from day one."

"Zack, you think everything is trouble," I reminded him.

He took off his baseball cap and twirled it on one finger. "Yeah, but this time I was right."

He was. We had to get the zombies out of our town, pronto.

"I say we concentrate on Chastity," I said.

"The girl is so high-maintenance, she takes up too much of our time. We won't be able to focus on the other zombies till we get rid of her."

"No way," Kyle objected. "Lassiter is a bigger problem. Remember what he did to Mr. Dubrowski?"

Mr. Dubrowski was working in the graveyard when Lassiter pushed him into an open grave. Although he recovered, the poor man had been treated in the hospital for a while. (We knew all about him because his daughter, Sara, goes to our school.) "But that happened before we even knew about the zombies," I pointed out.

Zack ran a hand over his brown hair. "So, what about the guy we saw today? He's going to need some time to recover, too."

"Lassiter is nasty," Kyle said. "He's done some major damage. He has to be our priority."

"I hate to disagree, but can I just point out that Penelope is bent on burning down my house?" Zack added in. "I know she means well, but she could end up being the most destructive zombie of all."

We started to argue back and forth, but Kyle put his hands up. "All right! They all have to go," he said. "Let's figure out how much we know about each of them, and we'll get rid of the one that we know the most about."

That made sense. We sat down on the front steps of the school, and Kyle opened his Freaky Files.

"I made notes on my interviews with Chastity and Penelope," he said. "But Lassiter hasn't been around, and I don't think he'd be up for a quiz. We don't even know when he lived."

"Chastity is from the early 1900s, and Penelope is from about thirty years before that," I said.

"We know each one of them has a serious problem that won't let them rest," Zack added. "Lassiter's seems the most serious. That ax in his back makes me think he might have been murdered. Maybe we have to find his killer and bring him to justice?"

"Yeah, but it all happened so long ago, the guy who killed him is probably dead, too," Kyle said. "I don't know, I don't see how we can send Lassiter back without his consent."

"I think Chastity's problem is that she's a bratty little slob," I butted in. "Maybe she has to learn how to clean up after herself."

"Well, if that's the case, she shouldn't be living with you," Zack said, laughing. "She won't learn a thing about cleaning up from watching you operate!"

"Ha-ha," I grumbled. "Come on, the bell is ringing. We'll figure this out at lunch."

I slid into my homeroom seat just before the second bell. I had to figure out Chastity's weak spot so I could zap her out of my life for good. But first, I had to deal with school. I like my teacher, Ms. Allison. She's a grown-up, but she's kind of a kid, too — one of those grown-ups who doesn't seem to have it all figured out, which is why I like her. She's got messy long hair that she pulls back in a ponytail, and she wears jeans and clogs to work. I'd love to be like her when I grow up.

"Okay, guys," Ms. Allison said. "Quiet down so I can make sure you're all here." She started taking attendance, and Matt Lopez turned to me.

"I saw Coach this morning," he whispered. "He said your mom called him last night and said you couldn't play in the game on Saturday. What's up with that?"

"Oh, no," I groaned. "I'm going to kill her. I've been trying to get out of this doofy party, and she won't budge."

"There's got to be something you can do," he said. "We really need you at this game. It's the Hurricanes, Amber. You're the only one who's ever scored against their goalie."

"I don't think there's any way out of this," I told him. "I've tried everything. I promise, I'll practice like crazy so I'll be really on top of my game next weekend."

Matt looked disappointed, like the game had already been lost. I felt horrible. "Come on," I told him. "This is your big chance to start. What if you play so well, you take my place as the starting center?"

"We're a team," he reminded me. "I don't want your place. I want us to win."

Great. Now I felt even worse. I barely heard another word out of Ms. Allison's mouth. And I didn't give another thought to the Chastity puzzle. All I could think of was the game I'd be missing.

I wasn't any closer to figuring things out by lunchtime. I hoped Kyle and Zack would have answers. But as I walked over to our usual table, I saw trouble: Tommy Hernandez.

There's nothing really wrong with Tommy. He's nice enough, but he's a complete couch potato. His favorite conversation subject is his Playstation 2 and the latest tricks he's found to push his high scores into total nerd status. The guy would rather watch TV than eat, though judging from his flabby frame, he does okay in the food department. Before Zack moved into the house between Tommy's and mine, I used to try to get him to practice soccer with me, but he was only useful as a goalpost.

Tommy was not up on the zombie situation. We were trying to keep our undead friends under wraps. Which was hard, because Tommy had a real nose for gossip, and he always wanted to be in on whatever was going on.

"Tommy!" I said, trying to sound happy to see him. "Don't you usually eat lunch with Chris and Colin Harris?" The Harris twins were computer-game champions. If working a joystick ever becomes an Olympic sport, they'll take home the gold.

"They both have a stomach flu," Tommy said. "They'll be out today and maybe even tomorrow. Dang, I wish I could stay home. I'll bet they got to level twelve of DragonQuest!"

Yeah, I'm sure that's worth having a stomach flu.

Kyle and Zack and I chomped on our sandwiches while Tommy babbled on about his latest game level. We kind of looked at one another, like "How do we get rid of this guy?" But there was no chance of losing Tommy without making him suspicious.

Already, his eyes drifted to the Freaky Files. Tommy and Kyle had been friends for years, but they bonded over computers. Suddenly, Tommy seemed way too interested in finding out how we were spending our time.

I was just about to ask Tommy if he was going to get the X-box when my eyes drifted to the window.

Oh, sheesh! My jaw dropped and a hunk of sandwich fell out of my mouth.

"Gross!" Zack said. "Amber, I don't like seefood."

But I was too shocked to answer. Out the window, I saw blonde hair and a white pinafore. I couldn't see her face, but I was sure it was pale, peeling, and halfway-rotten.

It was Chastity. What was she doing here?

CHAPTER SIX

A mber?" Now Zack sounded concerned.

I looked down quickly so that Tommy wouldn't notice my freak-out. There was my chewed-up lump of sandwich. "Gross!" I said. "My mom gave me bologna. She knows I hate it. I'm going to call her and give her a piece of my mind!"

I stood up and strode out of the cafeteria like a girl on a mission.

"I thought you loved bologna!" Kyle called after me. But within half a second, he and Zack were right behind me. Without Tommy. I guess Tommy was too excited about our leftovers to think about following us.

"What gives, Amber?" Kyle asked. "I don't believe your baloney about the bologna."

"Chastity is here," I told him. "I saw her through the window, just strolling along like she belonged here."

"Oh, no!" Zack groaned. "Isn't that one of the

bonuses of being undead? That you don't have to go to school?"

"No, it makes perfect sense," Kyle said. "In this one movie I saw, the zombies missed being alive and were drawn to the places where they spent time before they died. Chastity might sense the presence of all these kids. She just wants to be normal."

"Yeah? Well, me, too," I said. "And normal kids don't have to worry about — there she is!"

The huge double doors at the end of the hallway opened with a bang. Chastity walked through them, her wispy blonde hair flying behind her. The ragged trails of her dress brushed the floor as she turned right and wandered out of our view.

We had to get her out of here before some kid saw her.

We raced after her but, by the time we got to the corner, she'd disappeared. We split up, each of us taking a corridor. "Chastity?" I called quietly.

The only answer was a frantic yelp.

I followed the sound. Sure enough, it was Zack. No matter how much time he spent with the zombies, they always gave him a scare. He had Chastity in his sights, about halfway down the hall. Kyle found us a moment later.

"Of course!" I said, watching Chastity. "She went straight to Tiffany Schuyler's locker. How could she resist when it's decorated with hearts and glitter?"

"But what does she think she's doing?" Zack asked. "She can't break in there."

Chastity was fiddling with the lock on Tiffany's locker.

"Tell that to her," I said.

"Remember? She's got that zombie super-strength?" Kyle was already darting toward her. "Chastity . . . no, don't!"

But it was too late. Chastity's thin little arm ripped the lock off with a metallic snap, and the door swung open.

"Oh!" Chastity breathed. "So many shiny things!"

I ran up to her and grabbed her arm. "Chastity, cut it out!"

"Begone," she told me. "I want to see these lovely objects. They're so beautiful!"

She unzipped a makeup bag, peering curiously at the powders and potions inside. I grabbed it from her, and we had a momentary tug-of-war. Then Chastity glanced back at the locker — the girly treasure trove. She let go of the makeup bag, and I fell backward onto the floor.

"Ow," I said, rubbing my leg. "Come on, Chastity. Put this stuff back. It doesn't belong to you."

The girl didn't even hear me, she was so entranced by the barrettes, shiny bottles, and gloss pots in front of her. It was a pretty impressive collection. She picked up a pair of clips that had fuzzy pink balls hanging on ribbons.

"Ooh, pretty!" She gazed at them as if they were giant diamonds.

"Hey, what are you doing in the hallway, guys?" I heard a voice behind me. Oh, man. Ms. Allison. She's not a meanie, but she's still a teacher. She could bust us for being in the hallway without a pass.

"I had to go to my locker," I said, swinging the door all the way open so Tiffany's name was hidden.

"And we just wanted to come with her," Kyle added.

"So we could get our stuff. From her," Zack piped up. "Stuff she had for us. Books!" Boy, that kid needs some lessons in how to be cool.

Suddenly, I realized that Chastity was holding the two barrettes at her temples, shaking her head to see the pretty pink balls bob. Ms. Allison couldn't see her, but she could see the barrettes — and it would look like they were floating in midair.

I put my hands over Chastity's so that I was holding them, too. I pretended I was eyeballing them, trying to decide whether to put them on.

Ms. Allison blinked for a second. Then she took off her glasses and wiped them on her shirt. I guess she decided she was seeing things.

"All right, then get back to the lunchroom," she said. "I have to go sit down in the teachers' lounge. My blood sugar must be low."

She walked away, and we all let out a relieved sigh. I stowed the makeup bag back into the locker and grabbed the barrettes from Chastity.

"I WANT THOSE!" she shrieked in a furious voice, clutching them tight.

"Well, they're not yours," I told her. "Who do you think you are, anyway? You can't just take someone else's stuff. That's stealing."

"It's not fair," she said, letting go of the barrettes. "I don't have any of my own things."

"Are you thick?" I asked. "Chastity, I don't know how to break it to you, but most of your skin is rotting off and you don't even have enough hair for a ponytail."

I turned away from her. Tiffany's locker was hanging loosely on its hinges and was missing a lock. "We've got to fix this," I told the guys.

"I think we can nudge the door back in place," Kyle said.

I handed the barrettes to Zack, then helped Kyle push. Together, we managed to push the hinges back together. We swung the door closed just as the bell rang and kids started piling into the hall.

I wanted to get out of there as quickly as possible but, when I turned to get Chastity, she was gone. And guess who was standing there instead?

You guessed it. Tiffany.

"Amber McGee, what are you doing in my locker?" she demanded. Her perfect ponytail bobbed along with her head.

"I'm not in your locker," I told her. "I'm next to your locker."

"Which is totally missing a lock and broken," she said, fuming. "Were you trying to steal from me?"

"Oh, please!" I took off my baseball cap and raked back my curls. "It was already like this when I came by."

Tiffany folded her arms across her chest. "Right."

I could tell she didn't believe me. "I was just about to call the hall monitor to report this when you walked up," I said. "What would I do with your stuff?"

"Hm." Tiffany looked me up and down. "You're right. My stuff is definitely not part of your . . . your look. I guess I believe you."

Gosh, thanks.

"I can't believe someone broke into my locker," she said, opening the door. "Oh, no, they got into my makeup. Oh, and they took some of it! My foundation and powder are gone — and my lip gloss!" she wailed. She started pawing through the hair stuff. "Oh, no, my barrettes, the pink ones, they're gone, too!"

"Oh, no, I have those," Zack said.

We all turned to look at him. It was as if everyone in that hallway stopped to stare at

Zack, dangling the bobbly pink barrettes in his hand.

"And what are you doing with those?" Tiffany asked.

Zack's face began to turn red. "I uh . . . they fell out of your locker?"

Oh, Zack.

"Hmm, did they?" Tiffany glanced at her friends, who giggled with her. "Or did you reach in and get them when Amber found my locker open? Was it just too tempting?"

Zack held the barrettes out to her, his eyes wide. "I didn't take them!" he squeaked.

"Sure you didn't," Tiffany said. She turned to her friends, whispered something, and they giggled again. "You want to keep them? To remember me by?"

He shook his head like a frightened rabbit and dropped the barrettes in Tiffany's hand. "I don't need to remember you," he said. "I mean, I know who you are, and I don't, like, like you," he added. "I mean I like you, but not like that. I mean it's not that I like you. I mean you're a fine person, but you're not my friend. Not that I want you to be. But you're not bad. I mean . . ."

"We have to go," I interrupted.

The crowd was already hooting as Kyle and I dragged Zack away. Tiffany obviously thought he had a crush on her, and he was acting so goofy, I could almost believe it.

"Oh, boy," Kyle told him. "You're about as smooth as a cat's tongue."

"I can't believe she thought I took her barrettes!" Zack complained. "That was so embarrassing! I'm going to kill Chastity!"

"If we can find her," I said. "For a dead girl, she sure can move fast. Where do you think she is now?"

"I don't know, but if we don't get to class, we'll get busted," Zack said. "Which is worse — getting caught cutting class? Or leaving Chastity to roam the school?"

Now, there was a tasty choice. I didn't want to do either.

CHAPTER SEVEN

A ll right." I sighed. "I have study hall this period, so I'll look for her. You guys go to class."

"Your efforts won't go unrecognized," Kyle said, quoting from one of his favorite movies, *President Pod-Man*.

"Thank you, Mr. President." I waved goodbye, and they headed off to class.

My sneakers squeaked as I crept down the hall. I didn't want to risk running into another teacher. Especially Ms. Allison. If she saw me twice in one day, I'd be guaranteed detention.

I padded through the long, silent halls, watching carefully for any sign of movement in the distance. I heard a door slam behind me, and my heart thudded. I spun around to see Mr. Fletcher, the gym teacher, lugging some equipment across the hall.

Busted! I had to get out of there before he saw me!

I made a lightning-fast turn down the hallway to the left. The problem was, I didn't check first to see if the coast was clear.

"Hey, Amber!" a teasing voice greeted me.

Ugh! It was Parker and Rick, the two biggest pains in the collective neck of Paxituckett Middle School. While I was sneaking around like a criminal, they had cutting class down to a science.

"What are you guys doing out of class?" I asked.

"We could ask you the same question, Amber," Parker said. "Maybe you should make it worth our while not to say we saw you."

"Yeah, how much lunch money do you have on you?" Rick added.

"Well, since my mom makes my lunch, not a lot," I said. "Besides, lunch just ended, so if I had lunch money I would have spent it. You know, you guys are not the brightest gangsters on the block."

"Oh, so now you're going to defeat us with your super brainpower?" Rick laughed.

Something like that, I thought. Then I had a real brain flash. If these guys had been roaming the halls all afternoon, they might have seen Chastity.

"Say, did you guys spot a kind of . . . Well, have you seen a strange girl hanging around?"

"You mean, besides you?" Parker asked.

"Ha-ha. No, this girl is really different."

They looked at me like I had three heads. "You know what? Forget it," I said, and turned away. I'd find Chastity on my own. Even if it meant missing my afternoon . . .

There she was!

On the other side of the atrium, just inside the glassed walls, Chastity was yanking open the doors to the auditorium. Of course! Where else would such a drama queen go?

"See you guys later," I said, trying to look casual as I headed toward the auditorium. I had to get a hold of her.

I guess bullies can sense when someone's got a weakness. That's why they're bullies. Parker and Rick followed on my heels, asking where I was going in such a hurry.

"You going to try out for something?" Rick wanted to know.

"Step off," I told them.

"Is that Amber-ese for 'let's hang out'?" Parker asked Rick.

"I believe it is," Rick said. "We'd better stick

close to her, we don't know what she might be up to."

I sighed. I wanted to shake them, but it was more important to snag Chastity.

Then, I had a major brainstorm.

"Look, this girl I'm tracking down is my cousin from Los Angeles. She's an actress. Right now she's researching a part for a . . . a Disney movie. So if she acts kind of weird, don't freak out, okay?"

"An actress? From L.A.?" Parker sounded impressed. "For real?"

"Don't make a big deal out of it," I warned him. "This is strictly undercover. Okay?"

"I'll believe it when I see it," Rick sneered.

Inside the auditorium, I stood still for a moment, waiting for my eyes to adjust to the dark. I couldn't see Chastity, but I had an idea. Backstage, there was a big wardrobe room, filled with racks of clothes and mirrors framed by light-bulbs. That had to be where she was headed.

I strode up the aisle to the stage, where I hoisted myself up and went behind the maroon curtain. Rick and Parker followed me as if they were the Robin to my Batman. I pushed open the green room door.

Chastity sat at one of the mirrors, her back to us as she applied makeup from the drama club stash. Her wispy blonde hair tumbled down her back. She'd found a floppy hat dotted with cherry sprigs and she was wrapped in a deep red feather boa.

"Chastity, come on," I said. "We've got to get you out of school."

She blinked at me, then sniffed and turned away. "I'm not going anywhere with you. You're a horrible, mean girl."

I could see that she'd done a thorough job of applying pancake makeup to her face. With the help of Tiffany's blush pots, she might look halfway normal.

"I am not!" I said. "Anyway, you've done nothing but make trouble for me today."

"Just imagine," she said, ignoring my comment. "What if you were the one who had been dead a hundred years or more? How do you think your skin would look?"

Behind me, I heard a hissing laugh. "She burned you," Parker informed me. "You think your zits are bad, wait till you're actually dead meat!"

"Could you guys keep it to yourself?" I said. "Chastity and I need to discuss something."

"Oh, get off her back," Parker said. "She's really into this acting thing. Make her say more stuff about being dead!"

"Young man, Amber does not 'make' me say things," Chastity said, turning around and tilting her head at Parker. "And if you have something to ask me, you may address me directly."

"That is so cool!" Parker laughed.

Rick looked like he wasn't sure what to think. "How did she get her makeup to look like that?" he asked. "It's kind of weird. It really looks like her skin is rotten," he added in a whisper. "And it kind of smells funny."

"I apologize, all right?" I said to Chastity, giving Parker an exaggerated eye roll so he'd buy that I was just playing along with a difficult actress. "I should not have made fun of your skin."

"That's better," Chastity said.

"Now, will you come with me to study hall, so I don't get busted?" I asked her.

"Hmph." She seemed to consider my request. Then she shot Parker and Rick a flirty look. "Will these gentlemen be accompanying us?"

"I'll, uh, be your escort," Parker said, sticking his arm out so she could take it. I realized he was trying to talk like Chastity. "Allow me."

Oh, boy. This was a new side of Parker. Rick didn't seem too pleased. As for Chastity, she took Parker's arm politely, as if he were the man of her dreams.

The three of them followed me into the over-sized lecture room where my study hall took place. I signed in, and we went to a couple of desks all the way in the back.

"So, what's it like being dead?" Parker asked.

"It's dreadful," Chastity told him. "I spend my days and nights covered in dirt and dust. Do you know, I actually had worms on me?"

"No way!" Rick butted in. "That's gross."

"I detest all the mess," Chastity went on, "but if I don't return to the earth at least once a day, my strength just ebbs away. And then my skin looks even worse."

"So when were you alive?" Rick asked. "And what happened to you? Did you get murdered?"

"I did not!" Chastity snapped. "I would never be involved in anything so scandalous. I come from a fine family. I wouldn't want to besmirch my name."

Parker and Rick exchanged amused glances. "Your cousin's a scream," Parker told me.

"Right," I said sarcastically. But as Chastity

yammered on, I realized this info could come in handy. I pulled out my notebook and began writing down everything she said about her life.

"We lived in the Pines," she prattled on. "What a fine house we had! There were so many rooms, when a new servant would come, she would surely get lost just trying to change the linens."

"Yeah, the linens," Parker laughed.

"My mother was ever so beautiful." She sighed, clapping her hands. "And Papa had a handsome and manly bearing. Everything was absolutely perfect until . . ."

"Until you got murdered?" Rick asked.

"No, you foolish boy! Until the baby came. My mother gave birth to a little girl. After that, everything became tiresome."

"Yeah, tell me about it," Parker agreed. "My little brother never stopped crying for, like, a year."

"Exactly!" Chastity put a hand to her throat. "You truly understand me," she told Parker, and the guy actually blushed. Oh, brother!

"It was an extreme irony that my parents named her Melody, for her squalling had no music in it whatsoever," she went on. "I wanted nothing more than to escape, but I was supposed to assist in the care of this creature! As if I were nothing more than a servant myself."

Rick snickered. "Diapers."

"Yes, that was the worst," she said. "They were so wrapped up in the baby, they didn't notice when I began to sicken. By the time anyone fetched the doctor, it was too late: I was infected with pneumonia, and I weakened day by day."

"Pneumonia?" Parker asked. "You can die from that?"

"I coughed day and night," Chastity moaned. "It became hard to breathe. My lungs ached with the effort of it." Chastity brought a hand to her chest, reenacting her last days.

"Finally, I took to my bed. My parents tried everything. But there was nothing they could do. I weakened . . . I weakened . . . and then, the pain disappeared. My fever broke. I thought I was cured — but then I saw my mother collapse in grief. I was dead."

Chastity closed her eyes. My pen hovered over the paper, waiting for the moment to be over. For the first time I could remember, both Parker and Rick were silent.

"Whoa!" Parker said, finally breaking the

spell. "Dude, that was awesome! You're going to get an Oscar for sure!" He and Rick both clapped.

"Oscar?" Chastity blinked at them. "Who is this Oscar fellow?"

That made Parker and Rick laugh and clap even harder. Chastity couldn't help but smile at them. It was a match made in . . . well, they were getting along great.

Just then the bell rang, and I realized I had no idea what I was going to do with Chastity now. Study hall was one thing: As long as you signed in, nobody really watched you. But I had social studies next, and after that, a math test. Chastity would stick out like a sore thumb. And there was no way she'd keep quiet.

I was about to drag her outside and order her back to my house — as if that would work — when I realized she was still standing with Parker and Rick, chatting like any normal girl in school.

"Chastity, would you like to hang out with Parker and Rick till school lets out?" I asked her. "It'd probably be a lot more fun than going to classes."

"Hey, yeah," Parker cheered. "You can tell me

more about your character — I mean, your life," he said.

"Oh, man," Rick said. "You want to hang out with a girl all afternoon?"

Parker glared at him.

Then Chastity moved in for the kill. "Why, Rick, you needn't be jealous," she purred, taking him by the arm. "I assure you, a girl of my disposition can easily entertain two gentlemen callers. Would you like me to tell you more about the worms?"

Rick smiled reluctantly, and Chastity gave a tinkling laugh. Wow. The two most annoying guys in school, and she had them wrapped around her decomposing finger.

This was awesome. I had the rest of the afternoon to concentrate on school. Chastity was enjoying being the center of attention, and Parker was helping me without even knowing it. By dating a zombie! Other kids avoided him and Rick like the plague, so I could be sure nobody else would see her. Things were working out perfectly.

CHAPTER EIGHT

When the after-school bell rang, I met up with Kyle and Zack at the front doors.

"Oh, no, you didn't find her?" Zack groaned.

"Oh, I found her, all right," I told him. "Plus two assistants to watch her."

They looked at me as if I'd lost my marbles. So I marched them out the front doors to the bike rack. There she was, with Parker and Rick, swaying back and forth while she chatted with them a mile a minute.

"No way," Kyle said. "What's she doing with them?"

"They think she's my cousin, the actress," I said. "And they're totally hot for her."

"You matchmaking fool." Kyle laughed. "Excellent work."

"I hope she doesn't break his heart," Zack grumbled. "He'll blame you, and then we'll be watching our backs 24/7."

We disengaged Chastity from her new fan club. It wasn't easy. She wanted to stay — until I threatened to tell them just how old she really was.

"Oh, dear, I must go!" she told Parker and Rick. "But surely our paths will cross again. Good morrow!"

"'Bye, Chastity!" Rick and Parker shuffled their feet, looking pleased with themselves.

As we walked home, I thought I'd get to catch up with Zack and Kyle. But Chastity had an ax to grind. And it wasn't the one in Lassiter's back.

"You are a horrid girl," she told me. Then she addressed Zack and Kyle. "Do you know how horrid she is? She insulted me terribly today."

They shot me an alarmed look, and I just shrugged. Chastity tugged her new hat — the one she'd lifted from the drama department — down over her face. "She said my skin was rotten and . . . gross," she told them. "When I was alive, people used to comment on the loveliness of my complexion. They said I looked like a porcelain doll! I know I don't look my best now, but you didn't have to say it so bluntly."

I sighed. "I already apologized."

"And I am so bored at your house," she went

on. "It's filled with beautiful things that I mustn't touch. How frustrating! And my only companion is your mongrel hound. Why, even my baby sister was better company than a dog!"

"Leave Farley alone!" I said. "Maybe he'd be better company if you didn't try to dress him up all the time."

"I would think you would at least have a manservant or a housemaid," she went on. "I don't know how you function without one. Housekeeping is so dreary. Your friends Parker and Rick are amusing, at least. And so courteous! I wish I were staying with them!"

I gave a loud snort. "Parker and Rick? That's a laugh."

"They have better manners than you," she hissed at me angrily. I groaned. After everything I had done to keep her happy, she was going to cop an attitude?

"All right, we're home," I announced. "If I don't do some soccer drills, I may as well hang up my cleats for good. Chastity, you go with the guys."

"No!" Kyle yelped. I glared at him, but he was already backing away. "No way! Zack and I have to check on Penelope, and then we have to track

Lassiter in town. Who knows what trouble he got into while we were in school?"

"Don't you want to go with them?" I asked Chastity. "You just gave me the whole speech about how you hate spending time with me. Here's your chance!"

She gave me a shrewd look. "I have no wish to run across Lassiter," she said. "If they are going to meet him, I'll remain here. Besides," she added, "I shall teach you better manners. 'Twill be my quest for the day."

Uuuuugghh! Have you ever heard of anyone so annoying in your life?

"Fine," I stated flatly. "But stay out of my way. If I accidentally hit you with the ball, you'll probably lose an ear, and then I'll never hear the end of it."

The guys took off, and Chastity flounced over to my mom's flowerbed, where she sat in the dirt and smoothed mud over her arms. "I do the best I can," she told a mum. "It's not easy being dead and remaining beautiful."

"Maybe you should take a mud nap," I offered.

She ignored me completely. *Fine with me,* I thought. I got my soccer ball and dribbled it into the middle of the yard. My leg muscles felt a little stiff as I moved. It was like every bit of stress settled in my calves. But before too long, I loosened up and got into a groove, dribbling, kicking, and juggling the ball on my knees.

Then I did the ultimate soccer move. I read somewhere that one of my favorite players used to bounce the ball off his knee, up into the air, a hundred times a day. I try to do that, too, though I alternate between my foot, my knee, and my head. I was getting totally mesmerized by the soothing repetition of the boingy-boingy, up-and-down motion of the ball when I heard someone squeal and clap.

I turned to look, still bouncing the ball in the air, and saw Chastity watching me. She was grinning from ear to ear.

"Oh, that's grand!" she called out. "How do you do it? Is it magic?"

"Magic? It's practice," I told her. I gave the ball a little extra lift with my toe, hoisted it farther in the air, and bonked it with my head three times.

"Oh! You hit it with your head," she cried. "Doesn't that hurt?"

"Not if you do it right," I answered. I let the

ball come back down to my knee, then rolled it down to my foot, where I held it in place for a long moment. Then I popped it up in the air again and rolled it down my leg to the ground.

Yes, I was showing off. Can you blame me? It's the one thing I do well.

When I finished, Chastity skipped over to me. "That's terribly clever," she said. She kicked with more of a wallop than I expected. It traveled a good way across the yard.

"That was good," I told her. "But don't hit it with your toe. Use the instep — the inside of your foot."

"Why?" Chastity asked, giving a practice kick.

"The flat area is better for controlling the ball," I explained.

"Show me how you put it in the air," she asked.

"I'll show you, but it takes a ton of practice to get that right," I said. "First, you should learn to move back and forth with the ball."

I couldn't believe that girly Chastity was actually taking part in my soccer practice. Okay, partly she was just bored with sitting around. But there was something else. Deep down, she was just a kid. And undead or alive, kids like to play.

"Here, I'm going to kick it to you, and you stop it with your foot," I said. "Then you kick it back to me. Aim by looking at where you want the ball to go."

She gave the ball a whack with the side of her foot, and it whooshed powerfully toward me. I stopped it with my knee and kicked it back to her.

"OH!" she squealed, jumping out of the way. I was about to scold her when she ran back and got the ball. "Do it again," she commanded me. "I can do it this time."

Would you look at that? I thought. *The girl has some spunk after all.*

We kicked the ball back and forth until I worked up a sweat. Chastity had a natural flair for soccer. Plus, she had that zombie super-strength. Put the two together, and you get a really nice practice session. Before too long, she and I were as far across the lawn from each other as we could be, lobbing the ball long and hard.

"Whoa!" I laughed, catching one on my chest

and rolling it to the ground. "You trying to kill me?"

"If you think that was hard, wait for this one," she said, giving the ball a mighty whack.

I leaped over and caught it with both hands, landing with a thud in the dirt. So hard the air whooshed out of my lungs. I still had the ball, though. If I were the goalie, it would have been a great save! I rolled over and was about to hold it up triumphantly when a shadow crossed my path.

I looked up and got a nasty shock. Lassiter loomed over me, looking about ten feet tall from my spot on the ground. It's not like me to get scared, but the first thing I thought of was that awful whammy. I threw my arms over my eyes and rolled away from him. Then I sat up, ready to either run or try to fight him off.

But the big, ugly lug wasn't interested in me. He stormed across the yard toward Chastity. Just seconds earlier, she had been running and laughing. Now she looked more fragile than ever, a tiny waif. As he drew closer, she cowered.

That big bully. I hated him.

"You foolish child," he shouted in a thundering voice. "Running and playing as if you're still alive. You're not. You're dead!"

"Don't say that," Chastity said in a small, sad voice.

"You'll never be like them. You'll never be a living child again. Stop pretending. Can't you see what they are trying to do? They want you to disappear. They want to destroy you!"

Chastity backed up a few paces, but Lassiter was so much bigger than her. He reached out a big hairy mitt and grabbed her sticklike arm, shaking her.

"Stop this foolish charade," he commanded. "Stop trying to be like them and join forces with me."

Chastity stared at him, wide-eyed. I wanted her to look at me, so I could tell her we weren't going to destroy her. We only wanted to help. But somehow, the words stuck in my throat. Lassiter was so huge and threatening. Chastity was so small. Who could stand up to this big dead dude?

"Join forces with me," he repeated. "Together, our power is multiplied, and we can take over this world. Join forces with me NOW!"

CHAPTER NINE

I thought for sure Chastity was going to dissolve into trembling tears. But she had one more surprise for me. She stared at Lassiter's massive hand on her arm. When she looked up again, her eyes blazed with anger.

"You horrible bully," she spat. "Unhand me. That is no way to treat a lady!"

Lassiter glared at her. "You're not a lady," he growled. "You're nothing but a child. A child too stupid to know what's good for you."

"That's enough!" Chastity's commanding tone startled Lassiter. "Your manners are dreadful. And your brutish demeanor is unacceptable. No wonder you have an ax sticking out of your back. I'm sure one of your fellow woodsmen took offense to your deplorable deportment and sought to rid himself of you once and for all!"

Lassiter reared back and gave a roar of anger. He let go of Chastity's arm so that he could grab her by the throat — but she was two steps ahead of him. The minute she had an opening, she flitted out of his grasp and ran to me.

"The ball!" she shouted. "Amber, kick me the ball!"

I lobbed the ball over to her in a near panic. Lassiter was lumbering toward us like a big bear!

Chastity stopped the ball with her knee, just as I'd taught her. Then she turned toward Lassiter, setting up her shot. Mustering up every ounce of her zombie strength, she whaled on that ball. It shot like a cannonball straight at Lassiter's face — *POOM!* — and scored a direct hit on the big guy's nose!

Let me tell you, it was one of the greatest soccer moves I've ever seen.

"RAAR!" Lassiter screamed in surprise and pain. Chastity had knocked his nose off! He knelt down to pick it up before it turned to dust.

"Idiot child," he said in a pinched, nasal voice. "You will see that I was right and you will regret this!"

Chastity held her own nose and imitated his injured whine. "Idiot man, go take a mud nap so that your nose will grow back onto your face!"

Lassiter stumbled off. Chastity watched him

go, her hands on her hips. It was a totally new side of her. Instead of a brat, she was a girl who knew how to stand up for herself.

"That was awesome!" I ran up to her. "Way to heave the ball, Chastity!"

But she didn't share my sense of celebration. "I detest that man," she said to me, "and I do not trust him. But I must ask you. Was he telling me the truth about your intentions? Are you trying to make me vanish? Are you going to do to me what you did to Jeremiah?"

I swallowed hard. This was the moment of truth.

"It's not that we want to make you vanish," I explained. "It's just that we think we've found a way to send you . . . home. Back to your family. Wouldn't you want that?"

Chastity sniffed. "Return home?" she said. "Why would I want to do that? My parents have Melody to keep them company, and I certainly don't want to be around a crying baby who steals all the attention. I like this world. I like magazines and glitter body lotion. I have no reason to go anywhere."

Now, I'm an only child. To me, it seems like having a baby around would give my mom someone else to bother. But Chastity was really stuck on this baby problem.

"Let's let the matter drop," she told me. "Whatever method you have found to make me vanish, I'm not interested. I wish to play more of your soccer game."

She dribbled the ball away from me. I wanted to sell her on this never-never land thing, but what could I say? I'd have to work with the guys on refining my sales pitch.

We tossed the ball back and forth, and I noticed Chastity was really focused on the game. I knew how she felt. When I'm really mad about something, and I start to practice, I just feel my problems melt away. I guess she was doing the same thing.

Problem was, she overdid it. She gave the ball a really good kick, but she forgot to turn her foot so the instep hit it. Her toes squished against the ball, crackling.

"Ouch!" she shrieked. Chastity crumpled to the ground in a heap.

"Oh, man, you stubbed your toes," I said, running up to her. "That smarts. I know how you — EYUGH!"

This was a new one. Chastity unbuttoned her white kid-leather shoe and pulled it off her foot. She turned it upside down and shook it.

Out tumbled five toes! Totally gross!

"Oh, man, that's worse than stubbing your toe," I stammered.

"Truly, it is!" Chastity gathered her toes up in her hand and held them against her foot, just as Lassiter had just done with his nose. "Be quick about it, Amber," she said. "Go get me something to stick them back on with!"

I ran inside and opened the tool chest, but I don't think anyone's been in there since Dad left. The glue was all dried up.

"What's sticky?" I said to myself, running from room to room. "Come on. Give me something sticky!" I yelled at my house.

By then, I was in the kitchen. I'd left the peanut butter out on the counter. Well, it would have to do. I grabbed the jar and ran outside.

"At last!" Chastity said, eyeing the jar curiously. Clearly she thought I had gone bonkers.

"It's the stickiest stuff I could find," I said.

Without another word, she stuck her foot out, and I scooped big handfuls of peanut butter onto the stumps of her toes. Hey, I thought I'd seen gross when Ally Bandon tossed her cookies at camp. But this was definitely grosser.

It would be a long time before I would eat a PBJ sandwich again.

One by one, we stuck her toes back onto her foot, using the peanut butter as a thick layer of glue. When we were done, she leaned back and looked at our handiwork.

"I hope it heals properly," she said sadly. "I love these kid-leather shoes."

"Maybe you should go back into your mud bath," I suggested. "I mean, you went to school today, and then you played a good round of soccer. You're going to fall apart even more if you don't take a rest."

"How tiresome," she moaned. "I tell you truly, Amber, I detest muck and mud. And yet I don't feel right unless I sink my entire body into all that filth. Isn't that the most tragic situation you've ever heard of?"

"It sounds like a drag," I said, though I was eager to ditch her for a while. The peanut butter toes knocked it out of me.

"You are right," she lamented. "The only way to avoid turning to dust is to take my earthly sleep."

I helped her limp down into the basement. She held her peanut-butter foot carefully as she sunk into brown goo.

"How lovely," she said with a sigh, as if she were getting into a bubble bath. "When I forget it's mud, it's quite divine. I may stay here for an extra long time."

I watched her disappear beneath the surface of the mud and then heaved a huge sigh. Wow, I had some time to myself!

Farley and I ran over to Zack's house. The guys had just returned from their unsuccessful search for Lassiter. I gave them the lowdown on the big guy's temper tantrum.

"And that's not all," I said. "Big L has a plan for the zombies to join forces. He wants to take over the whole town."

"Can they do that?" Zack asked.

We looked at Kyle, who shrugged. "In *Dead, Deader, Deadest*, the zombies band together." He paged through his Freaky Files. "Right. That's the problem when zombies get together. They can pool their power. At least, in the movies they can."

"Great," Zack said. "Just great. A zombie megaforce."

"But Chastity and Penelope are not cooperating," Kyle pointed out. "So we've got nothing to worry about."

"Except . . ." I ran a hand over my thick curls. "Chastity is enjoying her stay way too much. I told her about sending her on, and she said she likes it here."

"More great news!" Zack covered his eyes with his hands. "She likes it here! We're doomed. Doomed to a life of zombie-sitting!"

"Eventually we'll grow up," I pointed out. "And we won't see them anymore."

"That is *so* not helpful," Zack said.

Just then Zack's mom came in with groceries, and we got up to help her. She's a college professor, but she doesn't seem stuffy at all. Hard to believe she teaches boring history.

"You kids look so serious," she said. "Did I interrupt something?"

"Actually, I've got to get home," Kyle said.

"Me, too." I punched Zack's arm. "Don't worry, Zack," I said loud and clear. "We'll figure out how to make those zombies disappear."

Kyle bit back a grin as Zack gave me a melting look. I knew his mother wouldn't get it, and I loved teasing him.

"Planning for Halloween already?" His mom asked. "Well, it's never too soon."

"That's what I always say, Mrs. Margolis," I replied with a straight face.

I laughed all the way home. Then I remembered that Mom and I were still sort of mad at each other. I thought about how to dodge her party as I started my homework. Then she walked in with a big bag of Chinese takeout — my favorite. I guess it was a peace offering, so I didn't bring up the party-versus-game controversy.

We were digging into our General Tso's Chicken when the doorbell rang. Imagine my surprise when I opened the front door and saw Parker Tolan standing there.

"What do you want?" I asked. "And where's your partner in crime? Is he out back, toilet-papering my mom's car?"

"No," Parker said. He fidgeted uncomfortably. This was seriously weird. I'd never seen him look so out of place. "I'm here alone. I just wanted to ask you something."

I could hear my mom tiptoeing over to the door to listen. I cleared my throat LOUDLY and heard her footsteps retreat.

"What?" I demanded. "Would you spit it out, Parker?"

"Is your cousin still here?" he finally blurted out. "Is she coming to school again tomorrow?"

"Not if I can help it," I told him. "Why?"

"I was just wondering. Um." He fidgeted again.

"What?" I yelled. "Parker, whatever joke you're playing, can you just get it over with?"

"I'm not playing a joke!" he said. Then he moved closer to me. "I was wondering if she likes me."

"Likes you?"

"Yeah. You know. Do you think she . . . likes me, likes me?"

Oh, brother. Parker had a crush on a hundred-year-old dead girl. This was too weird.

"Amber!" I heard my mom calling from the kitchen. "Why don't you invite your friend in? We have an extra egg roll."

"He can't," I shouted back. "He has to leave!" I turned to Parker. "You have to leave," I repeated. "I have no idea if Chastity likes you."

"Will you tell her I like her?" he asked. "I mean, if she likes me, I sort of like her, too."

"I'll tell her," I promised. I could hear my

mom coming and I didn't want to have to explain the conversation to her. "Now scram."

"Hi, Mrs. McGee —"

"'Bye, Parker!" I slammed the door.

"Amber!" my mom said. "That wasn't very nice."

"He had to get home," I explained. "He was in a big hurry."

"Sweetie, you don't have to be embarrassed," she said, peeking out the window. "He's cute!"

"Embarrassed about what?"

"About your new boyfriend," she gushed.

OH. NO. "He's not my boyfriend!"

"Oh, Amber!" My mom shook her head. "You're turning into a young lady overnight. First you're trying on my clothes, now there's a young man in your life."

"Mom. Seriously. I'm not kidding. Parker Tolan is not my boyfriend. He's so gross!"

"All right, whatever you say," she singsonged. "He's not your boyfriend."

I could see this was yet another losing battle. The more I insisted that the disgusting Parker Tolan was not my boyfriend, the more my mom believed that he was.

What was Chastity doing to me?

CHAPTER TEN

There I was, at the Women's World Cup. Thousands of fans cheered as I whisked the ball downfield toward Mia Hamm. She tried to block me, but I slipped past her. I was hot! I was fast! The roar of my fans filled my ears as I approached the goal.

"Amber . . . Amber . . . Amber . . ."

This was wild. The goal was, like, half a mile wide, and the goalie was the size of a Teletubby.

"AMBER . . . AMBER . . . AMBER!"

She shoots. She scores! And just as my team-mates hoisted me on their shoulders . . .

"*AMBER!* Wake up!"

My eyes flew open. The sun was just rising, pink in my window. Farley stood next to my bed with the fur on the back of his neck standing up. Chastity was shaking me.

"Would you wake up?" Chastity scolded. "Please. Stop dreaming, I must have a word with you."

"A word . . ." I muttered, wishing I could cling to my dream. Instead, reality slammed me. I was still a kid, the World Cup was years away, and I was stuck with this nagging zombie.

"What is it?" I moaned. "I'm so tired." I tried to roll over and close my eyes.

"Amber!"

I sat up and glanced at the clock and groaned. "Chastity, it is six o'clock. Why am I awake?"

"It's my skin," she complained. "Amber, look. It's even more rotten than when I went to sleep. I'm falling apart. You must find me some Orange Flower Skin Food."

"Skin food?"

"Yes! It was what my mother and I used to keep our skin soft. You don't have any?"

"No, I don't have any skin food," I said. Then I took a closer look. "Wow, you do look bad."

"Oh!" Chastity's hands flew to her face, and she ran to the mirror on my bureau. "I look awful."

"Sorry," I told her. "It's not that bad." I padded out of bed and stood next to her at the mirror.

"Woe is me!" she wailed. "Look at your skin. It's perfect, except for those dreadful freckles.

Next to you, I look like a . . . oh, dear!" Chastity was freaking out.

"Listen," I told her. "We know there's only one way for you to keep from falling apart, and that's to get in the mud and stay there."

She pouted at me in the mirror. "But I'm not tired."

"You don't know it, but you are," I said. Ugh, that sounded like something my mother would say. "If you were fully rested, your skin wouldn't look like that."

She turned to me. "Do you really think I look terrible?" she asked.

I looked her up and down. Stick-thin. Eyes that peered out from deep, sunken sockets. Wrinkly, rotting skin. Wispy blonde hair that barely covered her skull. "No, you don't look that bad," I lied.

"Oh, I'm so miserable!" she wailed. "I can't stand this shadowy existence. Death is so dreary!"

"Chastity, come on!" I had to tell her, like, five thousand times that she was pretty. I had to make up compliments that sounded so corny I thought there was no way she would buy them.

But she did. She soaked them up like a sad little sponge.

Then I thought of a new angle. "You know, there is a way that you could look young and pretty again."

"Really?" She sniffed. "Do tell me how! I'll do anything!"

"Let me tell you about when Jeremiah . . . moved on," I said. I told her about how we had solved Jeremiah's problems. "And in the minute before he moved on, he was restored to his young, true self. The guy glowed! Even his uniform was perfect."

She fiddled with the ribbons at her waist. "I don't know. I do wish to be pretty again," she admitted. "But I am enjoying this world of yours. I have gentlemen callers, new games, and . . . I like it here."

I sighed. "Well, think about it. You like being pretty . . . and having all of your fingers and toes."

She looked down at her foot with its peanut-butter surgery and nodded. "I must return to my mud bath."

By the time I had put fresh mud in the tub, I

was almost late for school. I had to rush like crazy to get out the door. But it was worth it. Chastity was planning to stay mud-bound for most of the day, so I was free to go to school without worrying about her.

I plodded to school half-asleep, feeling like a zombie myself. I caught a power snooze in homeroom. By lunch, I was feeling somewhat human. I met up with Zack and Kyle at our lunch table. It was just us, so we could finally talk about what we were going to do with Chastity.

"The girl has got to go," I told them flat-out. "I almost thought she was cool, but this morning's performance by the queen of melodrama burst that bubble."

"Well, let's go over what we know about her." Kyle pulled out his Freaky Files. "She's always talking about how rich her family was. And we know they lived in a neighborhood called the Pines."

"There's Eastwood Pines," Zack piped up. "When my family was shopping for houses in this area, the real-estate agent tried to get us to look there. But it was superexpensive. I guess it's still a ritzy part of town."

"Oh, duh!" I said, smacking my head. "Could that be what she was talking about? Were they old houses?"

"I don't know anything else," Zack said.

"You could call your dad," Kyle pointed out.

As I said, my dad is a real-estate developer. Of course he'd know everything about the area. I just didn't know how I was going to pull off my sudden interest in real estate. "I'll give him a call before soccer practice," I said.

"Other than that, we know that she had a little sister and that she died from a long illness," Zack said. "And that the Wells family was really rich."

"Oh, that's right!" Kyle turned a page in his notebook and showed us a note he had made. "My dad is representing a big investment firm called Wells, Rowley, and Carruthers. They've been in town forever. Maybe the Wells in the name is part of the same family."

"Could be," I said. "Can you check into that tonight?"

"You bet," he said. "A little Google goes a long way."

"Doing some background checking, Kyle?" a teasing voice interrupted us. We all looked up to see Tiffany standing there. She was flanked by two of her Tiff-ettes. "Is there someone you want to know more about? A certain girl in your school?"

She looked straight at Zack when she said that. The poor kid turned twelve shades of purple. "No, he's not," Zack said. "He's looking up something else entirely."

"I'll save you the trouble." Leaning on one hip, she batted her eyelashes at Zack. "If you type my name into a search engine, you get exactly six entries. The first one lists me as the star student at cheerleading camp — if you want a picture of me, that's a great place to start, Zacky-poo."

"Oh, cut it out, Tiffany!" I broke in. "You're so full of yourself."

"Ooh, look who's jealous!" she giggled. "Come on, girls. I don't want Amber to think I'm trying to steal her boyfriend."

That was twice in two days. Does everyone have boyfriend fever? For the record, I never, ever want to have a boyfriend.

Speaking of which, Parker almost smacked into Tiffany as she turned away from our table. She stared at him, dumbfounded. Parker hasn't eaten lunch in the cafeteria since second grade. The guy just wasn't seen here.

"Oh, hey, Amber," he said uncomfortably.

"What do you want with Amber?" Tiffany demanded.

"Nothing," he said.

She stared at him for a few more seconds, then gave me a curious look. "Well, you're certainly turning out to be interesting," she said, then walked off with her primpy posse. Zack shrank back in relief.

"So is your cousin here today?" Parker asked me.

"No," I said.

"Is she going to be here tomorrow?"

"I don't know."

"Well, are you going to see her after school?"

"Parker!" I snapped at him. "Give it a rest! I don't keep her social schedule."

He looked so disappointed, I almost felt sorry for the big lug. Kyle was amused, though. I guess the idea of an inter-life-span love connection was as funny to him as it was to me.

"Look," I told Parker. "I promise that next time I see my cousin, I'll mention you to her. Okay?"

"Okay!" Parker looked as happy as a little kid that just got a puppy. He almost skipped away. Too bad he didn't know Chastity was not my cousin. I was going to keep my promise, though. Next Christmas, I'd mention to my cousin Kelly what a pain in the neck Parker Tolan was!

"I wonder what he'd say if he knew her real story?" Kyle whispered to me as the bell rang.

"I don't want to find out," I said. "He's enough of a bully now. If we break the news to him, he'll never leave us alone. What a mess!"

"At least you aren't being stalked by the future prom queen," Zack complained. "Tiffany thinks I like her!"

"Well, if you don't stop blushing every time she comes near you, I'm going to start believing it, too," I teased him.

Hey, if I'm going to take it from my mom, it's only fair that I get to dish it out a little, too — right?

CHAPTER ELEVEN

I had practice after school, and I absolutely put my foot down and told the guys I was going — without Chastity. Even the most dedicated zombie-sitter needs a break.

The coach divided our team into two halves, and we played a scrimmage. It was great. The whole time, I was totally focused. But so was the other side. It was a tie, 0–0, and there were just a few seconds left on the clock. And I really wanted to score.

I focused on the ball and began running it down the field immediately. I passed it to Maria. She maneuvered it around the other team's offense and got ready to pass it back to me. I was right near the goalie net. It was a perfect setup. All she had to do was aim the ball for me, and I'd whip it right into the goal. It was easy as pie! I could do it in my sleep! I was ready to —

"Yoo-hoo! Amber! Over here. AMBER!"

Who the heck . . . ? Someone in a floppy hat,

sunglasses, and a rhinestone-studded jacket was waving to me from the sidelines. *Ohmigosh,* I thought. *Is that . . .*

The ball bounced past me and went out of bounds.

"McGee! Bench!" Coach pointed to the spot of disgrace behind him. He was clearly disgusted with me. So was I. But Chastity was still waving like crazy, as if she were on the deck of a departing cruise ship.

I plodded over to the sidelines. That was when I noticed Chastity wasn't alone. Zack was next to her — the rat.

"What's going on?" I asked. "You just ruined my practice!"

"Aren't you glad to see me?" Chastity said, peeking over her sunglasses. "I wanted to see how all that ball kicking worked with the rest of the team. It's very impressive!"

"Thanks." It's hard to stay mad when someone's complimenting your game. Anyway, the practice was over.

"Sorry," Zack said. "She woke up from her mud nap and, when we told her where you were, she had to see you play."

"What's with the fancy duds?" I asked, nodding at her hat and glasses.

"We borrowed some of my sister's stuff," he told me. "I just hope Trina doesn't notice."

"I think she has fabulous taste," Chastity said, whirling around. "This season's hottest looks feature shimmering shades of turquoise spotted with sequins and other special-interest details."

"You've been reading her fashion magazines, too, huh?" I asked.

"Well, of course! And I have the makings of a supermodel!"

I didn't want to go there. I took off my shin guards and put them into my backpack. Then I started to put on a warmer sweatshirt.

"Actually, I'm glad you guys are here," I told them. "I talked to my dad right before practice, and he told me where the Pines are. They're not too far. We can walk there now and see if Chastity recognizes anything."

"Oh, how clever!" Chastity cheered. "I told you this was a good idea," she scolded Zack.

"McGee, you want to join us?" Uh-oh. Coach was standing in a huddle of my teammates. I ran up and joined them.

"You guys are doing great with the hard stuff and missing the easy plays," he said. "McGee's goof was just one example. I saw you two do it, too," he said, pointing to two other players. "McGee, you're missing the game Saturday?"

"Yeah," I said, fidgeting uncomfortably. This was embarrassing.

"Well, if you're going to miss games, you can at least concentrate during practice," he said.

I felt about as small as an ant. From the way my other teammates were avoiding looking at me, I could tell they were disappointed with me, too. And I didn't blame them. I was distracted, my skills were off, and I was missing an important game.

"Sorry, Coach," I mumbled. He patted me on the shoulder, which just made me feel worse. But I couldn't worry about that now. If I wanted to get my life back, I had to get Chastity out of it. And at the moment, that meant getting her to the Pines.

I grabbed my backpack, and we were hurrying off the field when . . .

"Hey, Amber," a voice said.

It was Parker Tolan.

"Parker." I hitched up my backpack. "What do you want?" Not the nicest intro. But the big bully didn't answer. He just lingered, kicking clumps of grass.

"Hellooooo, Parker!" Chastity sang, stepping toward him. "Are you looking for me?"

"No!" Parker yelped. "I mean, not really. But, hey, you're here!"

"That I am," Chastity said, smiling demurely.

He grinned back. Zack stayed to the side, probably hoping Parker wouldn't notice him.

I frowned. "Chastity, we have to go."

"Hmm?" She gazed at Parker as if he were a giant lollipop.

"The Pines?" I said.

"Oh!" She snapped back. "Of course. I hate to run, Parker, but we have an appointment to keep."

"Oh," Parker said. "I thought we could see a movie."

"A movie!" Chastity clasped her hands. "That would be rapturous! Would we see a romantic comedy starring Jennifer Lopez?"

Note to self: Get those fashion and movie magazines away from this girl.

"Actually, I was thinking we'd catch a horror movie, *Zombies Walk at Night*," Parker said. "It's awesome. High gross-out factor."

Chastity hesitated. "Perhaps we can do something of that sort soon." She held her hand out.

Parker didn't seem to know what to make of her white gloves. He slapped her five. "See you around." Stepping back, he almost tripped, then waved as he loped away.

"I can't believe you turned that bully into a giant goon," Zack said.

I grinned, but Chastity looked sad. "He can never know my true story," she said. "He'll think I'm a vile creature from a movie. High gross-out factor."

"He's a jerk, anyway," I said, trying to be helpful.

"A charming jerk," Chastity said with a sigh. "But come along. I very much desire to see my ancestral home."

We took a shortcut across the woods and crossed the train tracks. When we came to the top of the hill, we could see the Pines.

This was the fanciest part of town. All the houses were more than a hundred years old, but they looked brand-new. My mom wanted to live here in the worst way. A smooth paved road wound through the rolling hills, connecting the mansions. Trees shaded them from one another, even though their manicured lawns were bigger than my soccer field. If Bill Gates moved to Paxi-tuckett, this is where he'd set up camp.

"Oh! There it is!" Chastity let out a gasp of joy. "That house with all the stones and the dig-nified chimney? It's mine. I'm home!" She turned to me. "Oh, Amber, thank you!" She gave me a bone-crushing zombie squeeze that left me unable to speak for a moment. Before I could mention that it wasn't her home anymore, she was running toward a big house at the top of the hill.

Zack and I chased after her, all the way up the hill. We were breathing hard, but Chastity didn't let up. She cut into the side yard, her skirts flying.

"Look, it's our gazebo," she called out. "Mother and I used to have tea parties out here. Oh, and this is where the pond was! They've made it into a garden. Papa set up a swing for me under this tree, that's gone, too. Oh, but the porch!"

She stepped up to the wraparound porch. Was she going in?

I sprinted after her. "Chastity, stop!"

"Oh, no," Zack muttered. "Houston, we've got a problem."

"Chastity, no!" I shouted.

But she wandered right up to the heavy wooden door, transfixed. First, she raised a fist to knock. Then her hand came down, as if she realized this was her house and she could go on in.

Except this wasn't her house anymore. And if she ripped that door off its hinges, the cops would come for sure. How would we explain that we weren't trying to rob the place?

She pressed her strong zombie hands against the door and shoved.

"Chastity!" I yelled at the top of my lungs. "Chastity, STOP!"

CHAPTER TWELVE

Zack sprinted past me, running like the wind. He threw the full weight of his body at Chastity.

But Zack just bounced off her like a fly hitting a glass window. He landed on his knees on the porch.

By then, I was on the porch, too. I squeezed in between her and the door.

"Chastity, this isn't your house anymore," I told her. "Don't break down the door. You'll get us in mucho trouble."

She stared past me at the door.

"Chastity?" I asked. "Did you hear me?"

She stepped back. Phew. She wasn't going to break down the door. At least, not yet.

"Come on, let's go home," I said. "How about a nice mud bath?"

But she didn't seem to hear me at all. She looked around the wraparound porch. She paced forward, counting her steps.

"Five . . . six . . . seven . . . eight," she murmured. Then she dropped to her knees and poked at the floorboard. When it didn't do anything in response, she whacked it with her hand. The wood splintered.

"That's gotta hurt," Zack said.

But Chastity seemed hypnotized as she yanked the plank up completely.

"Hey! Chastity, cut it out," I scolded.

She finally looked at me. "Well, it used to be loose!" She reached down, deep into the hole, and felt around.

"What are you doing?" I demanded. "Chastity, you're going to get us in such deep trouble, I can't even —"

"Got it," she said. Her arm came up, holding something. "Look, I found my things! Just where I left them."

Whoa. Zack and I dropped to our knees to check out the moldy, ancient tapestry bag she'd pulled out of the hole. She opened it and pulled out a porcelain doll. Its paint was faded and the clothes were matted, but I could tell it was super-fancy long ago. Chastity cradled the doll for a moment, then reached in again and pulled out a locket and a book.

"My diary," she explained, showing me the book. "This is where I wrote all my secrets. I hid it so that the prying eyes of the servants would never come across it. And this is the locket my parents gave me on my twelfth birthday."

Watching Chastity touch her long-lost treasures, I felt bad. Underneath all that rotten skin and even more rotten attitude, she was a lost kid with no family. I knew how much I missed my dad. If I lost my mom and a little sister, I guess I'd be pretty bratty, too. I felt sorry for Chastity. As sorry as I could feel for a pile of festering bones, anyway.

"Oh, please, I must go inside," she said, peering through the window. "That beautiful silver tea set . . . If I had such exquisite things in my mud bed, I would feel so much better about staying there! Please, I won't stay long."

"No way!" I insisted. "Come on."

"They're coming home!" Zack squeaked.

I heard the sound of tires crunching on gravel. He was right. A station wagon was pulling up in front of the house. A man and a woman peeked through the windshield. They must have spotted us on the porch!

"Come on," I whispered. "If we duck down

and run around the other side of the house, we can get out of here before —"

But Chastity stood up. Her eyes glowed with anger. "What are you doing at my house?" she demanded.

The people in the car had a white toy poodle with them. The poodle started barking furiously, but the people saw nothing.

"Chastity! Come this way," I hissed. "Come on, before the dog gets out."

But Chastity wasn't listening. Instead, she pointed her bony fingers at the car.

The whammy! She was putting the whammy on the couple in the car!

"Don't do that!" I grabbed her arm. "Chastity, that feels horrible. Take it off them!"

But it was too late. The couple sat frozen in their car. And I guess the effort it took to give a double-whammy was too much for Chastity. She put a hand to her forehead and sort of wavered in place. "I'm rather dizzy."

I thought she might fall, so I grabbed her by her arms.

"Are you okay?" Zack asked her.

"I must go," she said in a faint voice. "A nap, perhaps. I'm not well."

She clambered down the stairs, past the frozen couple in the car. Their dog was running back and forth between them, licking their faces frantically. He reminded me of Farley.

"Can't you unfreeze them?" I begged. "I feel so bad for those people, Chastity."

"I haven't the strength," she whispered as she stumbled away from the house. "But don't worry. It will wear off as soon as we venture away. When we get to the woods, they'll be fine."

The three of us booked. I did look back once we got to the woods and saw the driver's door of the car open. The man was on his feet, looking around. At least they were okay.

By the time we got home, Chastity looked much better. "Don't you want a mud bath?" I asked her.

"No, I'm all right now," she said, clutching her moldy bag.

"Wouldn't you like to hang out with Zack for a while?" I said. "He's such a gentleman, you know."

Zack snorted and punched me.

"No, thank you," Chastity said to him, as if he were the one who'd offered. "I'm feeling quite at home at Amber's house."

She walked ahead of me and through the open front door. My mom grinned, waiting for me to come up the front steps.

"Hi, Mom," I said as Chastity vanished into the house behind her. Mom gave a little shiver when the zombie brushed past her, then she squinted at me, beaming.

"I found your little surprise," she said. "I hope you don't mind."

"My little — what?" I asked.

She pulled a hand out from behind her back and showed me. It was a Barbie doll — a long-forgotten gift that I had never even touched. It was wearing a fancy homemade outfit made of colorful scraps. Probably from the rag bag.

"This is *amazing*," Mom gushed. "I didn't think you even knew how to sew. And you made such an intricate design! Amber, why didn't you show me?"

"Why?" I winced, staring at Chastity's handiwork. What could I say? That the fabulous doll gown came from beyond the grave? "Well, you're right, Mom," I said. "I wanted to surprise you. You like it?"

"I love it," she said. "It's wonderful, honey! I

set up my sewing kit so we could work on it some more. I want to show you how to make a dart, so her curves fit into the bodice. This is just like what my mother and I used to do!"

Oh, NO! Mom wanted to sit and sew with me all evening? I turned around and gave Zack a desperate look. *Help me!* I screamed silently. *Tell her we have a homework project to work on. Something. Anything!*

"Well, good night," he said, waving to me cheerfully. I made a mental note to kill him the next day. Then I turned around and followed Mom into the house.

This was going to be one big bore.

We sat at the dining room table, each of us with a Barbie doll. My mom worked on "my" Barbie, fixing the dress and chitchatting, while I fiddled with the other one.

"Well, go ahead," she said. "Don't be embarrassed. Make something," she said.

I stared down at the Barbie and thought how I could make a tidy little bonfire with her. But then Chastity sidled over to me. She sat silently to my right and reached across so that her hands were right in front of me. Then she began wrapping some silky material around the doll. She knotted it in the back so it draped over the doll. Cool. I shot her a grateful smile.

As Mom looked up, I put my hands on the Barbie. That way it looked like I was doing the wrapping. "That looks nice," she said. Phew.

"So, how's that mud project going? The one in the basement?" Mom asked.

"All right," I said. Glurf. Something else I had to fake. And something told me Chastity wasn't going to bail me out of that one.

"Mr. Strauss tells me that most kids haven't even begun thinking about their science project," she said. "You're really ahead of the game. I'm proud of you, sweetie."

"Oh, well, you know," I said. Then I thought about it for a second. "Wait. When were you talking to Mr. Strauss?" Was there a secret parent-teacher conference I didn't know about?

Mom blushed. "Oh. Well, I met him at the bank," she said. "We were both waiting for the teller at the same time. And we started chatting. And then we got some coffee."

Oh, no. I didn't like where this was going.

"Mom, you can't date Mr. Strauss," I said.

"We're not dating. Heavens. Where did you

get such an idea?" She pulled out a spool of thread. "You fly off the handle so quickly sometimes, and I hate to ruin this. Now that we've finally found something we can do together."

"Sewing?" I was less than thrilled.

"I've thought about starting a project like this together. Especially since your father left. I found myself wishing I could share things with you. Like I did with my own mother."

"You CAN share things with me," I said. "We could go running together. And when was the last time we rode our bikes down to the reservoir? You never come to my games. Why can't you do stuff that I like?"

Chastity glared at me and slammed the Barbie down on the table.

Mom looked at it, shocked. She thought I had done the slamming. And that was a seriously bratty move.

"If you're going to throw a temper tantrum, you can do it in your room," she said icily.

"But, Mom, I didn't —"

"Your room," she repeated, and stood up. She went into the kitchen and started banging the pots around. I wanted to defend myself, but I followed orders before I got into any more trouble.

Did I say trouble? When I closed the door behind me, Chastity glared at me, her hands on her hips.

"You, too?" I moaned. "What did I do now?"

"How dare you speak to your mother that way?" she demanded. "What does it matter to you whether you're making doll clothes or kicking a ball? At least you're doing something with her. At least you *can* do something with her. I can't. Because my mother is dead. And if she were alive, I'd never speak to her that way!"

My mouth hung open. I wanted to tell Chastity that no matter what, my mom should respect my interests. But the words stuck in my throat. What was the point of explaining it?

Plus, Chastity's words held some truth. I was mad at my mom — majorly mad. Why couldn't she work things out with Dad? Why did he have to leave? I was peeved at both of them and I was definitely taking it out on her. I could be nicer. Because I would hate to lose my parents for good, the way Chastity did.

Oh, man. Was I feeling sorry for her again?

With everyone in the house mad at me, it was going to be a long, long night.

CHAPTER THIRTEEN

'm sick of zombies," I snapped the next day. It was after school, and we were on our way to check out Wells, Crowley, and Carruthers. I was exhausted. I was in trouble with Ms. Allison because of Chastity. The zombie girl had decided the dream catcher hanging in my homeroom window would look better if it was hanging over her mud bed. So she "borrowed" it and put it in my backpack for safekeeping. When it fell out, I looked like the thief! Ms. Allison was "really disappointed in me."

Yeah. And I'm really disappointed in life, I thought.

"That dead girl is ruining my entire existence," I complained. "Zack, you've got to take her back!"

"No way," Zack said. "One zombie's enough for me. Penelope found a magnifying glass yesterday. She spent the afternoon burning holes into papers. My mom found them, and I almost got grounded because she thought it was me."

"Yeah?" Kyle piped up. "Well, I was just dropping off to sleep last night when I rolled over and caught Lassiter outside my window. On the garage roof! Just staring. That did it. No way could I sleep after that!"

"What did he want?" I wondered out loud.

"He still thinks we've got some magical way to get rid of him," Kyle explained. "When I opened the window and told him to split, he said no. Not until I give him the spell."

"Better keep him away from your notebook," Zack told him. "If he finds out we've got most of our information from movies and old episodes of *Buffy*, we're sunk."

Kyle hugged his Freaky Files closer to his chest.

"Enough terror talk," I said. "Look, we're here. WELLS, CROWLEY, AND CARRUTHERS, INVESTMENT FIRM," I read from the sign above the office door. "If Wells is still alive, we can ask him about Chastity."

We trooped into the office. There was a massive oil painting in the foyer. It had to be six feet tall. In it, a tall, serious old dude glared down at us. His eyes were the same pale blue as Chastity's. I hoped that was a good sign.

"May I help you?"

Beneath the painting, there was a big wooden desk where a receptionist sat. I hadn't even noticed her. She glared at us from behind thick cat-glasses. And the tone of her voice told me she had no intention of helping us.

"Hello," Zack said, stepping forward. "We're doing some research on prominent business people in town. It's for a school assignment. Could we talk to anyone in your company? Like Mr. Carruthers . . . or Mr. Rowley . . . or Mr. Wells?"

"Mr. Carruthers and Mr. Rowley are dead," she said.

"That never stopped us before," I muttered, and Kyle nudged me.

"And *Ms*. Wells has a full appointment book," she went on. "She doesn't have time to talk to children. Particularly children who don't do enough research to know she's the most prominent female business person in this town."

"Oh, my buddy here just got confused," I broke in. I took off my cap and shook out my curls, to be sure she knew I was a girl. "We knew that. In fact, that's why we're here. The report is about businesswomen, so we decided to start at the top."

The secretary nosed through a wide, imposing book. "I can make an appointment for next week."

"No way!" I squeaked. She cast me a sharp look. "I mean . . . the report is due next week. Couldn't we see her sooner?"

The woman folded her hands and pursed her lips. "Young lady," she said. "Procrastination on your part does not mean you can just waltz in here at the last minute and . . ."

"Sophie, are you scaring these kids?" a cheerful voice called out from behind us.

"Ms. Wells, these youngsters want to interview you," she said. "I told them they need an appointment."

"Sure, that would be great." The voice belonged to a woman who was surprisingly young. I mean, I guess she was about my mom's age. She had pale skin and fine, blonde hair. Right now, she was wearing a dark-colored suit. She had sneakers on, though, and her hair was held back in a ponytail. She was carrying a gym bag and a racquetball racquet.

"'Scuse me, kiddos," she said as she strode

swiftly past us. "I've got about a thousand E-mails to answer and I'm in a terrible mood. I just got killed by my lawyer — on the racquetball court, I mean — for the third time in a row."

"Well, it's no wonder, with that racquet," I blurted out.

That stopped her. "What do you mean?" She flipped her racquet. "This thing cost me plenty."

"Yeah, but it's totally designed for a man," I pointed out. "Nike has a whole new line out that's much lighter. It's ergonomically designed to complement women's strengths. I'll tell you about it — if you let us interview you today."

A smile spread across Ms. Wells's face. "Well, look at you," she said. "You're on. Sophie, bring some mineral water back here for me — and some OJ or something for . . ."

"Amber McGee," I said. "And these are my friends Zack and Kyle. We're working on the project together."

"Amber," she repeated. "Okay, guys. Come on back, and we'll chat."

We followed her to a humongous office. One wall was neatly lined with books. Another was covered with photos. The three of us sat on a creaky brown leather couch, with plenty of room to spare.

"I spend more time here than I do at my house, so I try to make it homey," she said.

"Hmm," I said. This place was about as homey as a library.

"Nice pictures," Kyle said, eyeing the walls.

"Mostly my family," she told him. "You can't do a report on me without mentioning them. My grandfather started this firm, and Wellses have worked here ever since."

"Your grandfather?" I asked.

"Yes, Arthur Wells," she said. "That was his mug you saw on the wall on the way in. Here he is again, looking a little younger. He's with his sister Melody at her wedding, just before he went to Yale."

We stared at the old, black-and-white photo together. Melody looked pretty, except for the doily on her head. And Arthur still looked serious. His pale hair was parted straight down the middle, and he had on a high, tight white collar. Melody had her little white hand around his elbow. They leaned close together, like they were the best of friends.

"So Melody was his older sister?" I asked.

"Yes. He was the third child in the family. The eldest daughter died in childhood." Ms. Wells leaned back in her chair. "I could go on about my family history forever. What was it you wanted to know?"

"Actually, this is interesting." I tried not to sound too excited. "Is there a picture of the older sister here?"

"Sure, over here." She grabbed a photo from the low cabinet behind her desk. "Here are Melody and Chastity, before Arthur was born. I was named for her."

"You're named Chastity?" I asked.

"Yes, there's a girl named Chastity in every generation of my family," she said.

I stared at her. The skin, the eyes, the hair . . . and the smile. I could see Chastity's beauty all grown up in this businesswoman of the twenty-first century.

And then, on the wall, I saw a portrait of Chastity.

"Wow," Zack breathed. "She was really pretty."

"Wasn't she?" Ms. Wells said. "Everyone talks about what a great beauty she would have been. Tragically, she died of pneumonia. Melody had only the barest memory of her."

Wow. I couldn't believe this was the pain-in-the-neck zombie who'd been ruining my life. I was used to her peeling skin and thin, brittle hair. But here was a photo of Chastity with smooth, soft skin, bouncy blonde curls, and the clearest eyes I'd ever seen. She was a living doll.

My mom would have loved her!

She must have been sick when the picture was taken. She lay on a bed, with Melody perched next to her. The baby's chubby legs stuck out straight in front of her. Chastity was wearing the gold locket, the one she was so crazy about finding. And Melody was clutching . . .

"That's a nice doll," I said cautiously.

"That was my great-aunt Melody's most prized possession," Ms. Wells said. "She talked about that doll until she died. It disappeared when she was small, and she . . ."

"She stole it!" I yelped.

Ms. Wells gaped at me. "I'm sorry?" Behind her, Zack's eyes opened wide with surprise. Beside him, Kyle nodded. He got it.

"I mean, she sold it," I said, lamely. "Maybe she sold the doll."

"Well, I doubt it," Ms. Wells said, looking at

me strangely. "I think she was only four years old when it disappeared."

"Oh. Just an idea. Well, thanks," I said, backing toward the door.

"I thought you wanted to interview me!" she said. "And what about my racquetball advice?"

"We have everything we need for our report," I said. "I mean, the couch, the pictures, the . . . desk . . . it all speaks volumes." Oh, my gosh, I sounded like an idiot. But I had to get the guys out of there and tell them the news: We had this zombie case sewn up.

"One more thing," I said. "Your great-aunt Melody. When did she die?"

"Oh, in 1970," Ms. Wells said. "She lived a long, full life. I loved hanging out with her when I was young. She was brimming with stories about the old days."

"And is she buried here?"

Ms. Wells nodded. "In her husband's family plot. She married a Carruthers, in fact. Our families are all intertwined. Say, why are you guys so interested in . . ."

"Thanks!" Kyle cut in. "Wow, what a great report we're going to write. Can we make a copy of this picture?"

"Sure," Ms. Wells said. "There's a photocopier down the hall. But what about our deal?"

"Right!" I went to her desk and started jotting Web sites on a pad of paper. "If you're looking for a great fit, check this out. And this second site will give you a great price. And the new women's racket is featured on this site."

She leaned over the pad. "Pretty impressive. Thanks," Ms. Wells said as Kyle returned the original photo. We said our good-byes, then ducked out of there.

Outside the building, Kyle and Zack stood there bug-eyed as I told them the key to the whole Chastity problem.

"Didn't you get that?" I said. "She was jealous of Melody, so —"

"She stole the doll," Kyle finished for me. "And the guilt has probably haunted her ever since."

"Oh, man! It's so obvious!" Zack said.

"Right!" I did a little happy dance on the sidewalk. "All we have to do is return the doll to Melody Wells Carruthers, and the Chastity problem will be solved!"

CHAPTER FOURTEEN

We got to my house in no time flat. The guys followed me down to the basement, where Chastity lounged in her mud bath. She was opening and closing her locket, watching it glitter in the sunlight. The doll sat at her feet, propped up near the bottom of the tub.

I picked it up. "Your doll, huh?" I asked her.

"And hello and good afternoon to you, too," she said in a cheerful voice. "Will you never learn manners?"

"Chastity, you don't have a bony leg to stand on," I told her. "Because the last time I checked, it was considered very bad manners to steal."

"Steal?" she sputtered, sitting up. "I stole nothing! That doll is mine. Mine!"

"Really?" I asked. "Then how come Melody spent the rest of her life wondering where it disappeared to?" I pulled out my copy of the photo and showed it to her. Chastity stared at it for a long moment. Then she sat back and burst into tears.

"Oh, my dear Melody!" she sobbed. "I am so sorry. I didn't mean to do it!"

"What didn't you mean to do?" Kyle asked in a soothing voice. "Tell us about it."

"The doll was just so beautiful. And I was so bored, lying in bed day after day, feeling my sickness overtake me. It all seemed so unfair. Melody was so sturdy. And loud! She had everything: my parents' love, her health, that doll."

"The doll you took," Zack pointed out.

Chastity ignored me. "One night, I awoke and everyone was asleep. I felt feverish and strange. I paced the house. I saw Melody's doll and thought, I'll just borrow it. When I'm feeling better, I'll play with it. I took it and hid it with my treasures. I did not know how sick I would get. I didn't think I would die before I could give it back!"

"You didn't mean it," Kyle told her. "You were just looking for something that would give you hope. That you would get better."

"I suppose," she said. "Although I must admit it gave me satisfaction to hear her cry when she found it was gone. My parents turned the house upside down in their quest for it. I thought it served them right for forgetting about me."

"Well, now we can make things right," I told her. "Just wait until tonight."

After dark, Kyle and I rode our bikes to the new section of the graveyard — the side that wasn't getting torn up by construction machinery. Chastity perched on Kyle's handlebars, and I have never seen anyone enjoy a night out so much. She whooped it up so loud, she must have woken up every kid in a one-mile radius. Ladylike? The girl could be a real tomboy when she cut loose.

When we got to the graveyard, I could see that they were almost done digging out the old section. "Look at that," I said to Kyle. "You can't even tell people used to be buried there. Pretty soon they'll be putting in the foundation for the new middle school."

"Yeah, they moved the old graves. But what about these dead people? They're supposed to rest in peace with a bunch of kids playing fifty yards away from them?" Kyle said.

"Probably one of my dad's brilliant plans," I said.

Zack pulled up a moment later on his bike.

He was wrestling with a giant backpack with thorny briars poking out of it.

"I hate this stupid rosebush," he complained. "It poked me the whole way up here."

"Well, we're going to need it," I told him. "Grab a shovel out of that shed and come on."

A map at the entrance told us where the Carruthers family was buried. Walking over there, we passed a lot of familiar names on the gravestones . . . old names from the town. We even went past Anthea and Benjamin Wells, Chastity's parents. But I didn't point them out. I didn't have time for a big woe-is-me scene from Miss Thespian of 1902. We found Melody next to her husband, under a big weeping willow. The dangling leaves shivered in the wind.

"Melody," Chastity breathed as she read the pale granite stone. "You lived so long! Well, of course. You were quite healthy." She gave a small laugh. "I can't believe she missed the doll for all those years. It makes me feel odd."

"Yeah, yeah," I said. "Less wigging, more digging." I handed her a shovel and dug into the ground myself. Kyle and Zack joined in, and before long we had gotten a good three feet down.

"Here you go." I handed her the doll. "Tell your sister you're sorry and give her back her doll."

Chastity hesitated. "You think this will make me become an un-zombie? That I'll move on, as you say?"

"I'm pretty sure," I said.

"Well. And I'll be beautiful again?"

I tried not to roll my eyes. "That's the plan," I told her.

"Well, I do feel that apologizing would be the right thing," Chastity said. "Charitable and proper."

"That's good, considering we rode our bikes all the way out here and dug this big hole," I said.

Now it was Chastity's turn to roll her eyes. She turned toward her sister's headstone. "Melody, I apologize," she said. She laid the doll down lovingly and gave it a last look. Then the four of us pushed the dirt back into the hole and planted the rosebush on top to cover up the recent digging.

We stood back and stared at Chastity.

"Well?" she asked. "What do you see? A golden light? Am I fading from view?"

"Um, sort of," I said, squinting. "Stand more in the moonlight, maybe that'll help."

She stepped to the side, away from the willow. "How about now?" She closed her eyes and reached up to the sky. "Let us commence! I'm ready!"

We all held our breath and waited.

Nothing happened.

"Oh, for crying out loud!" I kicked at a clod of dirt. "What now? What's wrong? Why isn't she vanishing?"

"I don't know," Kyle said. "Chastity, you felt bad about the doll, right?"

"Well, yes!" she said. "Of course, I did."

"Did you feel horrible about it?"

"Truly?" Chastity tilted her head. "Horrid is a strong emotion. It was never a large concern. 'Twas merely a doll."

I groaned. "Don't tell me this was a false alarm!"

Kyle touched his tie. "It's possible that a zombie could have multiple issues. Maybe there's something else she hasn't resolved." He patted down his jacket. "Wish I'd brought those Freaky Files. We need to regroup and rethink."

"Then I'm not going back?" Chastity asked. "I shall remain here?"

"Looks like it," Kyle said.

"Well . . . is that really so dreadful?" she asked. "Amber, I shall join you at school. Perhaps I could be in the play, as you pretended! In fact, with my help, you could become just as popular with the young men as I am. If only I weren't rotting! Amber, you must help me track down Noxzema. I saw an advertisement for it, and it's just what I need."

I opened my mouth to answer, when — whoa! Something was shaking the willow branches. I stared at them as they quivered wildly. A dark figure stepped out of the shadows.

A familiar figure with an ax sticking out of his back.

Chastity, Zack, and Kyle looked at me curiously. I pointed over their shoulders.

"It's Lassiter!" I shouted.

CHAPTER FIFTEEN

Did I mention that Lassiter is one big, nasty dude, even by zombie standards? His beard was matted and caked with dirt. His hair stuck out from his head in all directions. But his face was the worst. One eye missing, the other twisted with rage.

"You foolish girl!" he roared, lunging at Chastity. "I told you before. They want to trick you. If you join forces with me, we can overpower them and take over this place!"

"Not again!" Chastity yelled. "You awful man. I believe I made myself clear last time we spoke."

"But this time, I won't give you a chance to get away," he said. He reached down and grabbed the sleeve of Trina's spangled jacket.

"Let go!" Chastity demanded. She twisted around. She was trying to get her arms out of the sleeves. Instead, her hat plopped onto the ground.

"You won't get away this time," Lassiter

grumbled. He grabbed her hair with his other hand.

"Not my hair!" she shrieked. "Stop that!"

"You'll lose more than your hair if you don't stop that infernal shrieking," he ordered.

My friends and I were edging forward. I was ready to punch him in his muddy face, but then he reached behind him and yanked the ax right out of his back.

"Whoa," I said. "Put that thing down!"

"I was known to use this quite effectively in my day," he said, waving the hatchet at us. The cold steel glinted in the moonlight. Chastity gasped. He turned to her and held it close to her face.

"Strange, isn't it?" he asked her. "We spent so much time in the ground. And we are so cold. But the steel is still even colder to the touch, is it not?" He brushed it against her face.

I shuddered.

"Lassiter, let her go," I said.

"Would you rather feel the cold steel yourself?" he roared. The ax whooshed right past my face. I leaned back to avoid it. "Perhaps you want to join your new friend and sleep in the ground yourself?"

No, I did not. I stumbled backward and stood close to Kyle and Zack. The warmth of their bodies was comforting.

"Please, just run home," Chastity whimpered. "He can't harm me. Not really."

"Oh, no?" he asked her. "What if I chopped you into bits so that you turned to dust? You'd wander the earth forever as a ghost, without even the body you have now. No one would be able to see you, and you wouldn't be able to make your presence known. You'd be nothing but an invisible, useless wraith. I can make that happen. And I will, if you do not agree to join me!"

Chastity began to whimper. All her anger drained away, and she looked at Lassiter with real fear.

"That's it," I said, stepping forward. "Lassiter, let her go."

But he ignored me and dragged Chastity away.

I snapped on my flashlight and shot it in his face.

The blinding beam of the superpowered halogen lamp made him back up in surprise.

"Let her go, right this second," I barked. "Or . . . or . . ."

I thought fast.

"Or Kyle will use his magic box to send you back!"

Kyle stared at me. I nodded at the cell phone hanging on his belt. "Right, Kyle? The magic box? The one you got from VoiceStream?"

Kyle touched his tie nervously. Then he reached for his belt. "That's right," he said. He unhooked the little silver rectangle and pointed it at Lassiter.

"I'll just get the coordinates set." He flipped the cell phone open. "Let me see. If we are going to send this dude off, let me pick a really nasty place. Ah! Here we go."

He hit the RINGER-SELECT on the phone, and it made a shrill whistle.

Lassiter jumped.

"No, that's not it," Kyle grumbled.

"You need the X-20 modulator to be engaged," Zack said helpfully.

"Oh, you're right!" Kyle cheered. "Great. Okay. Let me get the transducer in order, and . . ."

"Stop that!" Lassiter did not look scared, exactly. But he eyed the cell phone suspiciously. "Put that away! Take the girl."

He let go of Chastity's hair and shoved her

forward. She fell into my arms. She kind of felt like cold meat.

"Foolish child," he said. "You should have joined me when you had the chance. You won't be able to, once I —"

Kyle's cell phone gave another whirring chirp, and Lassiter winced. "I'll be gone before your spell is complete. I'm too quick for your magic box!" He whipped his ax back and forth as he backed away. "But I'll be back. You've not seen the last of me!"

He backed away and disappeared into the shadows.

"Oh, Amber!" Chastity put her bony arms around my neck. "How clever! And, Kyle, you didn't fool me for a moment, but you were so fantastic! And, Zack, you've gotten very brave indeed."

Zack smiled uncertainly. "I'm not sure what to think. Did we just save a zombie from . . . another zombie?"

"Hey, teamwork rules," I said, slapping him five.

Kyle flipped his cell phone shut. "This is definitely a new chapter for Kyle's Freaky Files."

We said good-bye to Kyle and Zack, then turned up the street toward home. As we got closer, I noticed the glow at the end of the drive. It was my house — every light blazing.

"Oh, gracious!" Chastity said, brushing dirt from Trina's denim jacket. "Is there a party?"

"Oh, no!" I clapped my hands to my cheeks. "Mom must have looked in on me, for the first time in history!" I squeezed my eyes shut as it all played out. Mom had found Farley in my bed instead of me and freaked out. There she was on the front steps, clutching the keys to her car.

"I have been all over town looking for you! Where on earth were you?" she shouted, the minute I was close enough to yell at. "I was worried sick!"

Thank goodness she was out front, actually. What if she had caught me sneaking back in through the tree house? She would have had the whole tree cut down!

"I, uh . . ." The words stopped in my mouth. The quick-thinking Amber didn't have a clue how to get out of this one. I just stood there like a jerk with my flashlight and my bike. I almost wished she could see the zombie girl standing next to me, so she'd know I had a good reason to be out. But that wasn't going to happen.

"I left the house because I was feeling bad," Chastity said, standing close to me.

"What?" I asked.

"I said, where on earth were you?" my mother repeated.

I glared at Chastity, who pointed at my mom.

"Tell her you left the house because you felt sad and wanted to talk to your friends," Chastity repeated. "Just do it! Trust me, Amber. I've been watching your mother closely, and I know what she needs to hear."

This was insane. But I didn't have any better ideas.

"I woke up and felt bad," I told Mom. "I wanted to talk some things through with Zack and Kyle. So I woke them up, and we hung out for a while."

"I'm sorry I worried you," Chastity added, poking me with a bony finger.

"And I'm sorry I worried you, Mom," I added.

I stood there and watched. Mom looked down for a moment, then back up at me. The anger was gone from her eyes. Now she just looked sad. "Come here," she said. "I'm just glad you're safe."

Phew. Complete meltdown avoided. I walked up the porch steps and into my mom's hug. We stepped inside, and she brought me into the kitchen.

"I don't know what to do with you lately," she said to me as she put a teakettle on to boil. "I thought we were onto something with the Barbie clothes, but that only lasted a day. Some days you're as difficult as you always were, and then other days you surprise me and I think we can be best friends."

I felt my relief give way to a tightness in my throat. I turned away, wanting to shut her down. Gooey discussions were not my thing. I was ready to snap at Mom, but Chastity squeezed my upper arm. "Tell her," she said. "Tell her what you're really feeling."

I swallowed hard. "I want to be friends, Mom," I said. "But sometimes I feel like you won't let that happen because . . . because we're so different."

"We are different," Mom said. "But sometimes I feel as if you go out of your way to hate the things I love."

"I don't," I insisted.

Chastity rattled a teacup on the table. I held it still. "Okay, maybe I do, Mom. I know I diss your friends and . . . and a lot of things. But you know, I feel the same way about you. The way you hate soccer. The way you look at my hair and my clothes. You don't like anything about me."

Mom sat down beside me and sunk her fingers into the curls at the nape of my neck. "I love you the way you are, Amber."

Tears burned my throat. "Then why don't I ever feel that way?"

Mom pulled me close, and I pressed my cheek against her shoulder. It felt good to be a kid again, good to be her kid.

"Just because I criticize you, doesn't mean I don't love you, sweetie."

I waited for Chastity to blurt out an I-told-you-so, but when I glanced at her I saw that her eyes were shiny, too.

"It just frustrates me," Mom said. "I know I'm giving you good advice. And I'm definitely giving you all the opportunities I never had as a girl."

"But . . . that was then, and I'm different."

Sheesh! I could barely imagine my mom as a kid. "I have to make my own mistakes."

"Yes, I've seen that," Mom said wryly.

"And I guess I want different opportunities," I went on.

"Like the opportunity to get all muddy and waste time running around after a ball?" Mom asked.

"Mom, don't you read all the articles about girls and sports?" I answered. "I see them in your magazines all the time. It's not a waste of time. All the research says girls who play sports make better grades and get into less trouble."

She looked at me thoughtfully. "And you really enjoy it," she said. "You're not just doing it to get under my skin?"

"Oh, Mom!" Her face crumpled in such a funny way that I had to hug her again. "I'll admit that's a handy side effect, but it's not the reason I play soccer," I said. "I really feel great when I'm out there. Like I've got no problems and I can just focus on one thing."

"That's how I used to feel at ballet class," Mom admitted.

"See? It's the same thing — with different footwear."

"But can't you try to enjoy some of my things?" Mom asked me. "It can't be so horrible, coming to the country club and wearing pretty clothes. Is it really so bad?"

I sighed. "It's not that bad," I admitted. "But why is it suddenly so important to you that I do all that? You used to just shrug your shoulders if I didn't want to wear a dress. Now, it's like a huge deal for some reason."

"Well, it's just you and me now," she said. "I'm proud of you. And I want to show you off to my friends. And yes, I'd also like you to be a part of my world and experience things that eleven-year-old girls sometimes miss."

Oh, man. I hadn't thought of it that way before. "Oh," I said.

Chastity nudged me, but I didn't have anything left to say.

"I'd be honored to go to the party with you on Saturday," Chastity prodded.

Ooh! It would kill me to say that! So I changed it a little. "Okay. Now I see why you want me to go to the party on Saturday," I said. "No problem."

My mom looked up hopefully. Then she sat

up straighter in her chair. "Only if you'll let me be a cheerleader at your game," she told me.

"Mom!" Now I gave her a superbig hug. Not because I felt bad for her. Just because sometimes she could be the coolest mom in the world. "I promise I'll clean my nails and try to keep my hair out of my eyes," I said. "I'll even blow it dry."

"Oh, who cares?" Mom said, waving her hand at me. "If anyone asks why my daughter's hair is so wild, I'll say it's because she's a soccer champ, and that I'm proud of her whether she's wearing a dress or sweatpants."

I couldn't believe she was finally saying what I'd been telling her all along. Somehow I'd gotten through to her. No wait, *we'd* gotten through to her. After I hugged my mom, I turned to look for Chastity so I could thank her.

But the zombie girl was gone.

CHAPTER SIXTEEN

figured Chastity was at large in the house somewhere, so I didn't worry too much.

After my Mom and I had some of her minty-sweet tea, and we both went back to our bedrooms, I looked for her in the closet. No zombie. She wasn't in the basement, either. Farley didn't look too freaked out. Which was not a sign. He hated having her around.

Then it hit me. She'd been watching Mom and me — not just tonight, but for the past few weeks. It must have made her miss her own mother like crazy. That's why she was so into fixing my relationship with Mom. She really wanted to mend her own relationship with her mother. But it was too late.

Or was it?

I had a feeling I'd find Chastity out there somewhere. Probably at the graveyard where her parents were laid to rest. And after the help she'd just given me, I wasn't about to let her go it alone. I snuck out my window again — this time making extra-sure my mom really *was* asleep. With a few well-placed pebbles against Kyle's and Zack's windows, I got them out of their beds.

"Haven't you gotten into enough trouble for one night?" Zack asked me.

"I think Chastity's had a breakthrough," I told him. "I have a feeling this is the last time we'll be able to see her."

They rode with me to the graveyard, and I pointed toward the area where her parents were buried.

"Look, over there." Kyle pointed.

The night air was cold, but something seemed to glow amid the grave markers. A lone white figure stood there. She looked pale and eerie in the moonlight. Her head was bent down.

Dead leaves crunched under our tires as we rolled our bikes up to her. "You found me," she said, not looking up. "I didn't want to disturb you. I just wanted to come here. To see."

In front of her were her parents' twin graves. They had lived for thirty years after her death, dying within two years of each other. 'BENJAMIN WELLS, DEVOTED HUSBAND, FATHER, AND SON,' the first one said. 'ANTHEA WELLS, WIFE, MOTHER, AND DAUGH-TER,' was next to it. Both gravestones were tidy, made of gray marble.

"I was just talking to my mother," Chastity told us. "And to my father as well. I was a terrible trial to them. Always asking for more. Always making mischief with the servants and Melody. Never appreciating how lovely my life was until it was taken away from me. And then it was too late to tell them how wonderful they were."

"Wow," Kyle said. "That's a really nice thing for you to say, Chastity. I, uh . . . it's sort of surprising to hear."

Chastity gave a tinkling laugh. "Yes, I'm sure it is," she said. "I've been horribly selfish. Thank you all for taking care of me. Especially you, Amber. That is a simply wonderful mud bath you made for me."

She turned back to the gravestones. "Look at that," she said. "My mother's birthday would have been two days from now. If only I could be there to celebrate it with her."

I stared at the date on the gravestone. October 13. What was weird about that date? Why did it look so familiar? Was I supposed to remember it for some . . .

"Oh, no! That's MY mom's birthday!" I yelped. "Agh! I'm the worst daughter on the planet. No wonder the party was so important. And I don't have a gift for her or anything!" I smacked myself in the forehead. "Don't even talk to me. I don't deserve to live!"

Chastity touched my shoulder gently. "You can't be perfect," she said. "Isn't that what you and your mother just figured out?"

I groaned.

"Here. Would your mother like this?" She lifted her locket from around her neck and put it in my hands.

The delicate gold chain looked tiny in my palm. The clasp at the back was shaped like a tiny rose, and the locket itself was a work of art. Even I could see that. It was made of pinkish gold, surrounding a tiny pink porcelain heart.

"Mom would love this," I said to Chastity. "You know that. But you can't give this up. It's your favorite thing in the whole world."

She closed my hands around it. Suddenly her bony, clammy fingers didn't feel so bad. "Oh, a fat lot of good a bit of gold is going to do a dead girl," she joked. "Imagine, dragging a precious item like that into a tubful of mud. I want the locket to be worn by someone who will appreciate it."

I knew it was difficult for Chastity to give the locket away. I'll admit it, I got pretty choked up. Chastity wasn't a greedy brat anymore. She had grown up a little.

Suddenly, the locket glowed extra bright, as if the sun had come out and was shining on it. But it was still the middle of the night. "Did somebody turn on a flashlight?" I asked, looking up.

But the light was coming from Chastity.

"Oh, you're going!" I said, and Chastity looked puzzled. Then, as I watched, her skin became pale and pink. It pulled tight so that all the wrinkles disappeared. Her hair gently tumbled around her shoulders, shining and curly. Even her dress lost its ghostly wisps and suddenly appeared white and elegant. She looked just like the girl in the photo. But this time, I could see her in vibrant color. Her teeth glittered as if she were in a toothpaste ad, and her hair was the color of spun gold.

But the most amazing part was her eyes. Chastity blinked, and her dead sockets came alive. When she opened her eyes, the irises were the most brilliant turquoise color I had ever seen. They weren't pale or grayish, but a deep blue, like the ocean. Golden lashes sprung out around them.

Chastity smiled.

"You look like a supermodel," I told her, and she blushed. Then she turned, as if she'd just heard someone call her name.

Behind her, I saw two wisps of light wavering side-by-side. Kyle and Zack saw them, too. We just watched, amazed. Chastity lifted a delicate hand to wave good-bye, then she ran to the twinkling wisps.

"Her parents," Zack breathed.

For a brief moment, we saw Chastity enveloped by the two light figures. Then the three of them became so bright, we had to squint.

And then the light winked out.

It was just us in the graveyard, with cold blue moonlight instead of the golden glow. And Chastity was really gone.

CHAPTER SEVENTEEN

Goal!

I was dripping with sweat when I ran off the field. The game was almost over, and we were up by three points. Just in case soccer is not your sport, that's a crazy huge lead.

"All right, McGee," Coach said. "Are you sure you won't stay?"

"Got to go, Coach," I told him. "I'm sure you guys can take it from here."

I was glad we were ahead, because I had other fish to fry. I really wanted to get my hair blown out before the party. And then there was the matter of talking my mom into something a little cooler than the floofy pink dress she loved.

Mom gave me a high five when I climbed into the car. "Nice touchdown!"

"Nice try," I told her. "That was a goal. Touchdowns are in football."

"Goal . . . *goal* . . ." she murmured. "I'll remember that," she said. "We've got exactly an hour and a half before we have to be at the club. Think we can make it?"

"I know we can, Mom."

As Mom drove, the locket I had given her that morning glimmered in the little hollow of her throat. I smiled, thinking of Chastity. She would really love our salon adventure.

My mom pulled over to the curb in front of the salon and said, "Stay in the car for a minute. I have to run in and get change for the parking meter. If anyone gives you a hard time, just call the salon, okay?" She tossed me her cell phone and hurried away.

I watched her stride across the street, doing her high-heel run. Now, that was a trick I had to learn. Maybe.

Reaching into the glove compartment, I pulled out a Barbie doll. She was wearing blue jeans, and I was trying to design a jacket for her.

Yes, I got hooked on making the Barbie clothes. You got a problem with that?

As I fiddled with the fabric, I heard the train pull into the station, about a block away.

I looked up as the doors opened and people got off. There were a dozen or so passengers. But two of them caught my eye. Mostly because of their weird, stiff, old-fashioned clothes. Both people wore wide-brimmed hats and sunglasses. I squinted to see better. One of them pointed a bony hand toward the center of town.

A very bony hand!

"More zombies?" I said out loud. I watched them for a moment as they moved down the sidewalk away from me. One of them wore a long white coat like a doctor's. He limped along as if his bones could give way at any time. The woman had long, dark hair that swayed under her floppy hat. She wore a fringed skirt and moccasins.

I picked up my mom's cell phone and dialed Zack's number. I listened to it ring. And I watched the two figures approach a big, ugly dude.

A dude with an ax sticking out of his back.

"Hello?" Zack answered.

"You won't believe this," I said, as a wary thrill filled my chest. I took a deep breath and delivered the weird news.

"I think some other zombies just hit town," I told Zack. "We've got two more!"